"You actually sound like you care about what happens to me,"

Elizabeth said, relaxing against the pillows.

"Sure I do. You think I want to lose my creature comforts?" Cade kissed her, making it possible for her to pretend what he said had only been a joke.

"You'll be back tonight?" she asked.

"If you make it worth my while."

"You Yankee carpetbaggers sure have a lot of nerve."

"Yup, we're total opportunists." He was at the door, then turned. "Don't ever forget that, love."

"You're not joking, are you?"

"No, " Cade said solemnly enough to erase any doubt. "I'm not."

Dear Reader,

Spellbinders! That's what we're striving for. The editors at Silhouette are determined to capture your imagination and win your heart with every single book we publish. Each month, six Special Editions are chosen with *you* in mind.

Our authors are our inspiration. Writers such as Nora Roberts, Tracy Sinclair, Kathleen Eagle, Carole Halston and Linda Howard—to name but a few—are masters at creating endearing characters and heartrending love stories. Their characters are everyday people—just like you and me—whose lives have been touched by love, whose dreams and desires suddenly come true!

So find a cozy, quiet place to read, and create your own special moment with a Silhouette Special Edition.

Sincerely,

The Editors
SILHOUETTE BOOKS

JENNIFER WEST
Come Pride, Come Passion

Silhouette Special Edition

Published by Silhouette Books New York

America's Publisher of Contemporary Romance

To Alan, Judy, Steven, Scott, Tracey...
and Raffles Cohan. For all the good times shared,
and for those trips and treats to come!
With love.

SILHOUETTE BOOKS
300 East 42nd St., New York, N.Y. 10017

Copyright © 1987 by Jennifer West

ISBN: 0-373-09383-7

First Silhouette Books printing May 1987

America's Publisher of Contemporary Romance

Printed in the U.S.A.

Books by Jennifer West

Silhouette Intimate Moments

A Season of Rainbows #10
Star Spangled Days #31
Edge of Venus #71
Main Chance #99

Silhouette Special Edition

Earth and Fire #262
Return to Paradise #283
Moments of Glory #339
Object of Desire #366
Come Pride, Come Passion #383

JENNIFER WEST's

current hobby is tracing her roots to see if she has claim to any European throne. In the meantime, she writes novels, television scripts and short stories. Jennifer's husband, son, two Akita dogs and an indeterminate number of goldfish put up with her at their residence in Irvine, California.

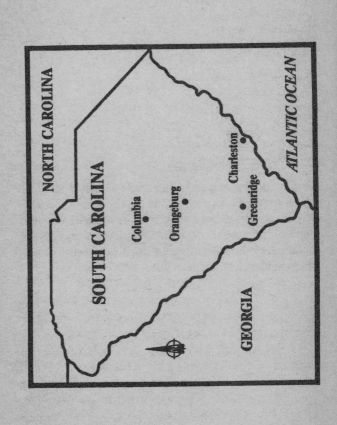

Chapter One

It was an afternoon filled with all the deep, easy contentment of a perfect summer's day: lazy blue sky hanging close enough to touch, air smelling of dark earth and mown grass, a sense of a hundred years of other summers holding just the same mood.

This was *her* country, *her* town, *her* world, thought Elizabeth Hart with proprietary satisfaction, as she strolled beside her husband. Up ahead, across the field over which they walked, flags flew on high standards atop the roofs of small, gaily colored tents. Like the wings of birds they lifted and fell in the thermal breezes. An old Confederate flag was stationed stubbornly beside that of the United States, and between both poles an enormous relic of a Civil War cannon had been trundled to a rest. To Elizabeth, the tableau of the old merged with the modern bore a poignant sweetness and underscored the afternoon's pervasive mood of elegant continuity.

Next to her, Edward Hart waved to Jake Fenster. Fenster owned the town's lumberyard. His family had lived in Greenridge almost as long as Elizabeth's, and through longevity and wealth, the Fensters prevailed as a part of the Hart's social set. They were, however, never truly considered "one of them," and were more or less just tolerated.

Automatically, and with scant feeling, Elizabeth smiled. She saw that today Fenster's corpulent frame was housed in a blue-and-white-striped seersucker suit. Red-faced, with his neck already speckled with pinpricks of heat irritation, he rambled along holding a collection of helium-filled balloons.

"You come by the Rotary booth, now," Fenster called jocularly, "you'll get your balloon." His eyes slid away from Edward and refocused on Elizabeth. In a voice almost imperceptibly thicker, he said, "Elizabeth's so pretty, she's gonna get herself two!"

On cue, Elizabeth smiled again, her true feelings of revulsion submerged beneath her standard of etiquette.

Fenster reminded her of a salivating dog. His fleshy, partially smiling lips were moist, as if he might like to make a quick meal of her. His pale blue eyes were similarly watery and hungry as they raked over her form.

In the presence of Fenster, and those like him, she was ever thankful of her marriage to Edward. Without Edward in her life, wolves and jackals would surround her at every turn. From her divorced and widowed friends she knew well enough the lament of the unattached female. The code of the Southern gentleman was merely given lip service; beneath the outer courtliness lay the same greedy lust that spilled from the pores of Jake Fenster.

He joined them, and the three walked together as a group. As Edward and Jake exchanged recent news of local doings, Elizabeth's mind flew backward. She was a girl of five—even then naturally poised—walking with her parents over this same land; then ten, drifting beside her father, this time consciously aware of her natural elegance; and finally a composed young lady of sixteen, who crossed the field with friends speaking of parties and prep schools and possible fortuitous marriage alliances, and occasionally, in breathless voices, of the secrets of sex. And on this summer's day, in those same, familiar surroundings, she was a woman of languid self-possession, a splendid creature of femininity, as fully ripe as the season.

"Elizabeth, careful..."

Edward's warning came too late. She stumbled slightly in a shallow rut, but righted herself instantly.

"All right?" Fenster asked unctuously, beside her. His hand had come up to clasp her arm. Elizabeth pulled away from his hot grip, using a laugh as a means to break their physical contact. Inwardly, her flesh crawled.

"Only feminine vanity injured," she said lightly.

"No matter what you do, you always cut a pretty picture," Fenster oozed.

Annoyed, Elizabeth said, "Oh? Well, I'm sure the tongues of some of our finest citizens are probably already wagging." Amazed at her own uncharacteristic venom, Elizabeth cut off the rest of what she had been about to say.

"It's the heat, darling." Edward smiled down at her. But the message in his brown eyes contradicted the outer warmth. She was not behaving with impeccable social grace; she was not behaving like herself. And it was true, although she did not know why. Perhaps it *was* the heat.

"It's the heel of this ridiculous shoe!" For the day's occasion she had worn new, elegant white leather heels, inlaid with flowered designs of white snakeskin—admittedly not the sort of footwear best suited for negotiating a field used each summer as a parking lot for the hundreds of cars driven to the Greenridge Fair. But it was important, given her position, to dress her social part, and Elizabeth made a special point of vigilantly upholding her image, seeing it as a duty more than a vanity she had jokingly embraced.

Edward linked her arm in his, steadying her over the uneven terrain until they reached the flat ground of the fairground proper.

There they parted ways with Jake Fenster.

"You come by the booth, don't forget, Edward."

While speaking to Edward, Fenster was looking with lascivious intent at her. There was no indication that Edward recognized the man's interest. But lately Edward had seemed more detached, more disconnected from everyday concerns—she had almost chosen the word "reality." Instead, her mind had skittered over it. Reality, or lack of it in this context, seemed dark and heavy, a swirling, bottomless pit of a world into which a person's life might fall.

Several times over the past few months, she had attempted to engineer earnest conversations with Edward, discussions she had hoped would illuminate the change in his personality.

She wished that she, too, could lightly dismiss the recent aberrations in his behavior and personality to the heat, but it was not possible. In her wildest imaginings, she had thought he might be involved with another woman. There were nights when he did not come home until the early hours. There were days leading into full weeks, when he did not want to make love to her. There had even been shameful moments when she had thought of following him. But the thought of doing that was so humiliating that she could not succumb to carrying out this indignity.

Fenster was backing away, balloons bounding against each other over his head. "And you, too, Elizabeth. You come by for your balloons."

Elizabeth tried, but could not manage a smile. She found herself staring blankly at Fenster. She did not look at him, so much as absorb all that he was. Fenster: the man represented a part of life she had both avoided and, by way of her privileged birthright, been spared. There was a baseness to him, a brutal ugliness. It was as if her impression of reality contained all that was beautiful and refined, and his contained the mirror opposite. Looking into his eyes, she saw that other world reflected back at her. It was not the heat, it was Fenster who had caused her to act against her usual standards of conduct. Elizabeth shuddered and looked away.

When she turned back, he had left. The original sweetness of the day returned to her.

With Edward, Elizabeth explored the labyrinth of booths and tents. The soil was covered with new, sweet-smelling wood shavings. In a few more days the curls and pieces would turn dark and grimy from being trod upon by the thousand or so visitors, but this afternoon the strips of wood were the color of clear, light honey. That Elizabeth's hair was the same enviable shade was a comparison not lost on others who turned curious, admiring and jealous eyes in her direction as she passed by.

Now and then Edward would pause at a charity booth and speak to an acquaintance. Elizabeth stood beside him, laughing when appropriate, remaining quietly reflective at other times. Her role as wife to the county's wealthiest industrialist was a part to which she had been born and bred. She did not see it as tiring, nor as unfulfilling.

On the summer of her twenty-eighth year, should anyone have had the bad manners to ask her, she would have said honestly that she was happy with the content of her life.

And then it happened—the terrible thing, the unthinkable, impossible event.

In one stupefying moment, her idyllic life was irrevocably shattered.

Chapter Two

Cade Delaney's stomach tightened as he looked through the rental car's windshield, his green eyes traveling ahead down the length of the wide boulevard bearing the prosaic name of Main Street. It was quiet now, in the heat of the summer's afternoon, but Cade saw it as it had been a long time ago on a winter's day, when the mill had been the most important in the state. Just as he had done on that last afternoon, Cade swallowed down the bitter taste of hatred.

The time he remembered had been thirteen years ago, and now he was thirty. Thirteen years! His father had died three years after they had left Greenridge—died a broken man, as the saying goes. An apt saying though, for in the strictest sense that was how it had been. In one way, Cade considered his mother lucky for having died earlier. At least she had been spared the horror he and his father had lived through in the town she had called home. With his father, he had buried her in the town cemetery, with a few neighbors who had loved his mother in attendance.

His mother was the reason for his trip back this Sunday afternoon. After leaving Greenridge he had never looked back, never trusted himself to return for fear of what he might do. But thirteen years was a long time, and the callow seventeen-year-old small-town boy he had been then was now a man of thirty with a graduate degree in business from Columbia and his own management consulting firm. He was a sophisticate, a New Yorker, a man who had buried hatred and passion and pride in the flat coldness of ledger sheets and time-and-motion graphs. Or so he had thought.

Now, as he drove down the wide tree-lined avenue of his youth, the old rage once again tore at his insides, and he knew he was not yet safe from the past. He wondered if he had been right to make this journey after all.

The trip had been an afterthought; no, he reconsidered, more of an "under-thought." For, if he were honest, he would have known that somewhere in the shadows of every sleepless hour he had spent over the years was the guilt of not returning to see his mother's resting place. There was also, Cade supposed, the guilt stemming from his fundamental cowardice. He had not had the guts to come back to Greenridge and finish what his father had started.

Well, he was back; passing through, but he had returned, nonetheless, to the scene of all the many crimes. The pilgrimage was, in truth, only a side trip. It had been precipitated by a consulting job he had acquired in Charleston, a two-hour ride down the highway through the low country. Tomorrow night he'd be on a jet heading back to Manhattan, perhaps not to return for another thirteen years; perhaps never to return at all.

He saw there had been little if any change in the town since he had left. It was an easy matter to locate the cemetery, with nothing more than his memory for a guide.

Amid the marble edifices and granite slabs, some dating from the eighteenth century, he found the small mound of his mother's grave. The headstone seemed smaller, even more insignificant than Cade had remembered. He spent an hour there sitting on a neighboring tombstone and speaking silently to the mother he remembered as kind and gentle, as deserving of more than she had ever gotten in life.

For a while he was a small boy again, slamming through the wooden screen door of their back porch, running into her open arms. Good times, they were. The sugary scent of baking cornbread had filled his nostrils. Sunday dinner after church was fried okra and chicken and sweet potatoes, and a winter's rain sluicing down the roof brought hot chocolate and a hug. She had made a thousand ordinary moments special because she was special.

He hadn't brought flowers. Nothing was open that Sunday. Instead, he left a piece of his heart as he knelt at the grave and said goodbye.

As he drove out of town, his thoughts were thick, moving like molasses through his mind. He had gone fifteen minutes out of his way before he realized he had taken the wrong direction. This knowledge hit him in the form of a great white house, its neo-classical columns as stately as they had been before the Civil War. A stand of ancient live oaks lined either side of the wide graveled approach to the mansion. From their boughs, moss trailed like the filmy lace handkerchiefs of Southern belles.

There was no sign of the occupants about, and Cade slowed, finally coming to a stop in the middle of the blacktop. Wave upon wave of images and emotions assaulted him as he stared at the building.

It was here that Proctor Huntington, his father's persecutor, had lived and dined on roasts and drunk imported wines and plotted filthy deeds. It was here, in this hub of luxury, that a web had been spun to choke out his father's life.

Cade threw the car into gear and sped off, blinded by a white rage that obliterated all reason. He flew down country lanes, careless of the speed, wanting to wreck his life once and for all and end the guilt, stop the torment of memories that surfaced whenever his guard was let down. *Years ago, he should have done something.* He was the son. He had been the hope of the father to right the terrible wrongs. Only he hadn't.

He was thirsty and hot when the brightly colored flags broke the placid horizon. The Greenridge Fair was in full progress. Cade remembered that, too—how it had been when he was a boy. There would be the rented rides, the smell of cotton candy and booths manned by the town's finest citizens, selling goods for charities to benefit the very people who purchased the canned fruits and crocheted doilies. There would also be something cold for him to drink.

It was good that he had stopped. The confusion of the crowds turned his mind to other matters, and for a while he was content to drift along the serpentine route of handcrafted goods and games of chance, where stuffed teddy bears with pink button eyes glared malevolently at children wishing to take them home.

And then Cade saw her.

As if walking through a tunnel of time, she approached. At first she wasn't real to him, only a vision, but then, hadn't she always been that, a girl not quite of his world? Untouchable, unfathomable, unforgettable, he had thought of her on countless hot summer nights or frosted mornings as he lay in bed. In these waking dreams he had imagined how she would feel and taste and smell.

Elizabeth.

Just as she had been the object of his most heated fantasies, she was the daughter of his father's enemy, the very flesh and blood of his father's destroyer. Another of life's cruelties.

The paper cup holding the orange drink sweated in his hand as, transfixed, Cade took her in.

At first he had not noticed the man. She moved along beside him. Now and then the man would stop, and she would wait by his side.

Cool, she looked, even in the afternoon's heat. The man was dressed in white trousers and a light blue jacket. His manner was not quite arrogant, but went beyond mere composure. When he turned fully toward Cade, Cade recognized him. The face and body had fleshed out, but it was unmistakably Edward Hart. Hart had been five years ahead of him in school. His father was not rich but ambitious, and had infused the son with that same urge to conquer. He had won at everything: sports, school elections, even charity drives. And, lo, hadn't he won the Lady Elizabeth, too?

Cade did not know at that moment if he felt satisfaction by proxy for Hart's accomplishment in obtaining Elizabeth as a kind of ultimate prize awarded for hard work and unrelenting drive, or if he wanted to kill Edward Hart right then and there and carry off the lovely Elizabeth as booty to be ravished.

So lost was he in his lustful thoughts that for an instant he floated in a surrealistic world where inner and outer merged crazily, even as the horror took place.

It was as if God had clapped. From out of nowhere, the sound came loud and sharp and final.

Cade watched it as a drama unfolding: Edward's face smiling...Elizabeth, turning to her husband, also smiling...neither of them understanding what had already occurred.

Then the smile on Edward's face dimmed. It fell away as the red stain seeped through the material of the shirt, blood spreading onto the blue jacket, flowing onto Elizabeth's white suit, even as she screamed Edward's name and fought to hold him up, even as he—like the smile—slipped downward.

There were shouts, some screams.

The past surged forward in time for Cade, as he recalled another day when he was seventeen and shots had been issued.

From the corner of his eye, he saw the hand come up again and the weapon thrust outward. He saw the curl of lip, the animal hatred etched on the man's face.

Cade lunged. He brought his hand down in a modified karate chop against the assailant's wrist. The weapon fell and the man screamed out in pain or surprise.

Elizabeth turned toward him at that same instant. Cade was caught in the blue of her gaze. Unable to free himself, he floated in an infinite expanse of depthless water, flew through a majestic sky having no boundaries.

"Elizabeth," he whispered, the gun and carnage forgotten.

He thought she searched his face, that there was something of recognition or a question in her look, but in the next second a rush of bodies filled the space between them.

The killer—for Edward Hart lay dead on the golden sawdust—was apprehended.

Instantly, Elizabeth was surrounded. She was sobbing and choking down screams of despair and denial. She thrashed out at her captives, and once managed to fling herself across Edward's supine form. Gently, she was removed.

Cade watched, unable to go to her, unable to leave. It was always the same for him with Elizabeth.

A doctor arrived and took over her management.

Cade thought of intervening as she was led away. But to what purpose? To say he was sorry? She would not hear him, nor would she remember.

The doctor fought to clear a path for her through the small clusters of horrified friends and idle gaping spectators. She passed so close to Cade that he could smell her perfume. The seductiveness of her scent was somehow a shock in the obscene circumstances.

Her face was splotched with tears and dirt, yet even in her frantic condition, she was amazingly, exquisitely beautiful and his body ached as he watched her move like a slow dream through his line of vision.

Elizabeth. She was still his inherited enemy, and still his desire. In thirteen years, nothing had changed. Nothing ever would.

A roar rose up, and Cade looked to the source.

Several men had begun to pound on the killer. Ugly shouts rang through the crowd. His first instinct was to rush into the fray and defend the man against the violence. But that was crazy; the man had just murdered another man. It was the brute ugliness Cade wanted to end, the men were only incidental.

Cade backed off. He pushed his way through the pandemonium, sickened. He was still trembling as he climbed into his car.

The violence had both horrified and inflamed him. It had resurrected a passion for revenge so intense he felt he would explode from its force.

That night he stood at the window of his hotel suite and looked out over the city. He was calm now, and safe. He had spent several hours engaged in rational thought. Never could he trust himself to return to Greenridge again, where passion and greed and hate—and the tantalizing promise of fulfillment—floated on every passing breeze. No, the past belonged where it was: let all the dead lie.

Chapter Three

In the first days following Edward's death, she would awaken in the mornings, and as always for a split instant there would be no thought at all. Then her mind would move, and comforting thoughts of Edward and the day's anticipated schedule would crowd her mind. But in the next beat, as she turned her head to the empty pillow, the peace would explode into the new and terrible reality. Edward was gone.

And with Edward's death, a whole way of life seemed to similarly dissolve. All that had been solid in her existence now appeared without substance; all of what had seemed to be timeless and lasting, she suddenly realized, had never been other than transitory. It was as if the world she had lived in was no more than a stage setting, which now, piece by piece, was being dismantled and carted off. She alone remained, on a bare stage, without a role to play.

A few weeks after the funeral, as the calendar edged toward the end of July, another rude fact had to be faced upon waking. She could no longer support the pretense of financial solvency. There were corners to be cut.

The sorrow seeped through her bones with every step, yet with the practiced, easy grace of an entire lifetime, Elizabeth moved across her expansive living room toward the housekeeper, whose own fortunes were about to be altered. A prearranged mask of dignity hid the deeper emotion of humiliation from the older woman, who anticipated their conversation with dark, accusing eyes.

"Good morning, Aggie," Elizabeth greeted.

"Good mornin', Mizus Hart," the housekeeper replied. Gone was the usual deference in tone and attitude.

The great bank of tall windows fronting the house were open, and in the silence of the surrounding countryside Elizabeth's heels clicked loudly on the dark hardwood floors before touching down silently as her path took her over an Oriental carpet. Its geometric and floral background was a dark wine red. Elizabeth had always found it to be a pleasing accent to the room. Now, the crimson stain reminded and mocked. Elizabeth shuddered at its sight and a momentary wave of vertigo washed through her, just as on that day at the fair.

"You're all right, Mizus Hart?" Aggie asked, with a disinterest that canceled the statement of concern.

"I'm fine. Just the heat. I must remember to take a salt pill today."

Aggie nodded, remaining mute.

Ordinarily, the response would have been more effusive. But Elizabeth knew that Aggie blamed her, as she might a traitor who had brought about disaster through conscious intent. Employment was not easy to come by in Greenridge. Neither were husbands, thought Elizabeth, bleakly. A part of her even identified with Aggie's antagonism. There were times when in her own irrational, totally senseless way, she blamed Edward for leaving her alone in the world.

"Weather's bound to break soon," Aggie commented dourly.

"Yes, it's due, isn't it? The storm." Elizabeth's attention drifted beyond the windows. An expanse of emerald green lawn, mowed yesterday by a small tractor, stretched out from the wide front veranda.

For days it had been oppressively humid. As if attending to some ritual, great white clouds assembled every morning. By afternoon they darkened into bulbous shapes whose shadows cast a net of gloom over the landscape. Then sometime during the night the weighty forms would lumber away, their ponderous exits occasionally punctuated by a sonorous bellow of thunder and a few sizzles of lightning. In the daylight, the pattern would repeat, still with no relief gained.

"River might overflow," Aggie said. "Could damage the crops, too. Could likely make a right mess of things. Lot of people are worried."

"Are they?" Elizabeth had forgotten the outside world. She listened to Aggie with amazement, as if she were a traveler in a foreign country, long cut off from outside news. So, the world beyond the velvet expanse of lawn still existed. She used to live there. But things had changed, hadn't they? Now she didn't live anywhere but in her thoughts, and then only in the past most of the time.

"I'm sure you understand how sorry I am about this," Elizabeth remarked, looking down at the white envelope in her hand.

Aggie said nothing, merely stared, as if passing silent judgment on a living example of hypocrisy. Elizabeth could almost see phrases of rebuke form behind the black eyes. Over an iced tea, Aggie would lean forward and tell a friend all about Elizabeth Hart's stupidity and selfishness and how it was likely she deserved her sad state of affairs. Later that friend would repeat the tale to another acquaintance, who would eventually relate the matter to one of Elizabeth's own friends, who would shake her head and cluck, "Such a tragedy." And more calls would be made. Elizabeth knew very well how it would go; after all, there had been times in the past when she, too, had said about someone else, "Such a tragedy."

It had always been Elizabeth's habit to wear dresses, and that, at least, had not changed since Edward's death. She had kept herself up, if only to lend some sort of purposeful activity to her life. The routine was comforting. But somehow, under the circumstances, she wished she had had the foresight to put on slacks, something less blatantly in contrast to the situation. In a dress costing as much as Aggie made in a month, she was about to explain how she could no longer afford the woman's domestic services. The cook and handyman had already been let go, and yesterday the two gardeners who tended the orchard and flower and vegetable gardens had been dismissed.

She felt like an alien in her own home, even in her body. Her hair was generally a buoyant mass about her face, but it drooped as listlessly as her spirits. And although not ten minutes out from her morning shower, the beige silk shirtwaist dress clung like clammy fingers against her skin. She longed to tear the dress from her body. She longed to have this ordeal over. She would fling herself unclothed against the pink silk sheets of her bed and cry. She would beat her fists and rail in fury and grief over this ultimate blunder orchestrated by Fate. She would exhaust herself and when she awoke, the cruel mistake would be no more than a terrible dream. Edward would be back. Her life would be intact.

"I'm just surprised, is all." Aggie accepted the proffered envelope from Elizabeth. It contained her salary and severance pay.

"No more surprised than I am," Elizabeth said back.

"Well, you could have known."

There it was at last, the accusation. The sentence whipped against Elizabeth, cutting into her ego like a wet leather strap. "Known? What? That Edward would be shot by some maniac?" she replied angrily.

"About the money. About running the house. How can there be nothing left?" Aggie demanded, her thin lips pursed prissily together. "All this and there's nothing left?"

"That's none of your concern, is it?" Elizabeth snapped. She was not accustomed to being reprimanded by anyone, least of all by a hired woman.

Aggie gave an unpleasant laugh. "Not anymore, I guess." She looked at Elizabeth, scrutinized her coldly, then turned and found her way to the front door.

Her hand went to the handle, but abruptly she turned back and marched through the entry hall to the edge of the living room. "That man, that 'maniac,' used to work at your husband's mill. He got fired, too. No one cared about him, neither." She paused. "Welcome to the real world, Mizus Hart. Hope you like it just fine."

"I'm sure I'll manage."

Aggie shook her head as one might dismissing a hopeless situation. With a parting shrug, she took her leave.

Elizabeth remained where she was, frozen in place by the white-hot anger radiating through her. The woman was a monster. The world was ugly. She didn't want any part of it. Only now she had no choice.

As for the people of her own social set, Elizabeth found them to be most kind during the initial stages of her bereavement. Bereavements were, after all, ultimately a form of social entertainment, like a barbecue or a black-tie dance. In Greenridge, life among Elizabeth's peers revolved around such affairs. They had for over a century, and neither the Civil War, nor the First and Second World Wars had done much to dim the town's appetite for such idle events. Elizabeth supposed the trend would continue for another century at least.

Besides the changes in her immediate world, she sensed her own internal transformations as the days passed. There was an irony to her outlook that had been absent before. Increasingly, since Edward's death, her thoughts had taken on a bitter, astringent quality, previously foreign to her nature. But there was so much now that was equally unfamiliar in her present life.

For one thing, as Aggie had prophesied, she really was poor. Edward had never tended to life insurance. After all, he owned the mill. The mill would provide all the security they would ever need. Or so he had said.

But Elizabeth found nothing but financial knots and snags when she investigated drawing income from that source. There were liens, she was told. There were release forms. There were any number of reasons why she could not get her hands on any cash to sustain her. It was a hopeless mishmash of financial double talk, but the bottom line seemed to be "No money." There was, according to what she could make of the situation, no "liquid capital" to be had. And that was that.

When she insisted that there had to be money there— or how could Edward have supported them—there were lowered eyes and snuffling and dissembled replies. There were, however, no real answers. Out of it all came one certain impression: she was a woman—only a woman—and as such should not consider such matters her domain.

"As a woman, then, I am going to starve to death!" she exploded in the bank's office.

No one liked it that a woman raised her voice. She had not known that before, because she had never had to make a demand. A raised voice was ugly. They all but said so. People did not like a woman to be ugly.

Everyone—including Elizabeth—wished she would, or could, just go back to being the way she had always been.

Eventually, as the days wore on, the social circus manufactured by her widowhood took on a mundane quality. Friends seemed to resent her new status, as if it were a virus she might spread. As the weeks progressed, the calls dwindled. If some miracle did not occur, Elizabeth projected that in a few months she could easily be destitute and all but forgotten. The idea of being out on the streets was still as totally unbelievable as Edward's demise.

She bought popular magazines, magazines she had never looked at before that were dedicated to making the lives of working mothers and single women more fulfilling.

At night in bed she would pore over such articles as "How to Ask for a Raise and Get It" and "Stretching a Four-Piece Wardrobe into Sixteen Different Outfits" with the incredulousness of a blind man suddenly given sight. Afraid and frustrated and angry, she would fling the magazines to the floor, wondering where she had been all those years when other women were stretching wardrobe dollars and shopping for four on a one-income budget! And more importantly, where was she going to go now? She was a twenty-eight-year-old woman who had just descended from an ivory tower into a pit of muck.

Welcome to the real world, Mizus Hart. Hope you like it just fine.

"Damn," Elizabeth said, remembering Aggie's smug countenance. And then she laughed. She had never said the word before. She said it again, and it sounded good. It felt good, even. She laughed so hard she rolled into a ball on the bed, clutching her sides. And somewhere in the middle of it all, she began to cry, until a sob turned into a scream and her voice cut through the lonely corridors.

"You look lovely tonight, Elizabeth." Mason Philips stepped into the entry carrying a bouquet of red roses.

He did not look like Elizabeth's idea of a white knight charging to her rescue, but as owner of the bank holding the mill's loans, he might be just that. And she was not in a position to leave any white knight unturned.

"Thank you, Mason. It's nice that you could come."

"I much prefer to conduct our relationship on a social basis, Elizabeth. You know that, I'm sure."

"I do, Mason. I do."

She invited him into the living room, and excused herself while she put the flowers into water. His eyes followed hotly after her. That was all right: let him look. Certainly, being obviously assertive—a new word she had picked up from recent explorations into worldly literature—had done her no good. Being sneaky might.

Her dress for the occasion had been selected with care. The cocktail dress with a neckline aptly described as plunging, was of deep blue satin, its color matching her eyes. Worn long and full, her light hair just touched the delicate shoulder straps. She was the picture of femininity.

Oddly, in spite of all the misfortune in her life, she had felt, as she surveyed her impression in the mirror earlier that night, that she had never looked better. Grief had given her a certain edge, lacking before. Whereas she might have been considered beautiful in a kind of vapid beauty queen fashion in the past, there was now a depth to her expression. In fact, lately she had become quite fascinated by herself in a morbid way. It was as if she were watching a transformation occur—one which was happening on its own and which she was helpless to control. There was a line at her brow, which she was certain had not been there before Edward's death. And her cheekbones were higher, or at least more pronounced, the fullness eaten away by worry. There were times when the changes—both inner and outer—frightened her, and she wished to cling to the phantom of the past and stave off the arrival of this new persona whose influence was gaining on her every day.

But she couldn't. Life had gotten out of control. Life was happening to her.

"I guess you know I've had to let Cook go," Elizabeth said. "So you're in for it tonight. A roast. Hope you like it medium. The oven seems to have conked out on me in the middle of everything else." Actually it hadn't. It was one of the few things to have remained operational in her life. But it sounded good, or rather, bad, and that's what tonight was all about—misfortune and pity, and getting her hands on some money.

"Elizabeth," Mason said. "You can't imagine how this all pains me."

Elizabeth lowered her blue eyes. "You can't imagine how grateful I am to know that someone cares about me." She raised her blue eyes to look into his. "It's dreadful being so helpless."

"Well, perhaps I can help," Mason said quietly. "Perhaps I can solve all of your problems."

Elizabeth let matters rest for the moment. There was no sense in overkill. The night was still young. Actually, she was not certain of the demarcation lines between overkill and assertive and aggressive. Maybe if she read enough magazines, she'd become sufficiently enlightened. She wondered how many issues it would take to become caught up in the ways of the world. In the meantime she would have to feel her way along the uncharted territory. What she did know was how to lower her eyes and smile and remain quiet for long intervals. After her recent weeks of battling to be heard as a person, it made her quite sick to do so, but she thought the circumstances necessitated a certain degree of compromise.

There were candles on the table as well as the roses that Mason brought. The meal was punctuated by long, manufactured silences and demurely lowered lashes, and after the dessert Elizabeth suggested they retire to the veranda, where it was cooler.

"I love this place." Mason surveyed the moonlit landscape from the edge of the porch.

"Yes, so do I," Elizabeth said truthfully. "Oakwood's belonged to my family for a long time."

"Since the early eighteen hundreds," Mason added crisply, as if proud of his scholarship. "A fine, fine home."

"I only hope I can keep it."

"You can, Elizabeth, you can."

Elizabeth waited, but he said no more. Taking up the slack, she said, "I only have five thousand dollars left to my name, Mason. Barely enough to pay for food and lights and—"

"You shouldn't think about money, Elizabeth."

"I know, Mason." She almost laughed, but it really wasn't all that funny, not when the irony of the statement touched one's life in a disastrous way. Instead, she sighed. "I do pray, but so far my prayers have gone unanswered."

"Not so." Mason turned to her. "I'm here, aren't I?"

Elizabeth waited, curious to know where this whole melodrama was going to lead. By the look on his face, she had an idea it might be upstairs.

It wasn't exactly that Mason wasn't an attractive man. He was closer to her age than Edward had been, and had there not been such a driven quality to his personality, coupled with an air of calculated coldness that seeped through the layer of outer charm, Elizabeth felt she might succumb to the longing she read in his expression.

"Mason . . ."

"I know it's soon . . . but—"

"It is."

"I'm sorry. But you're so very beautiful. It's only natural."

"I'm flattered, but . . . I . . . Edward . . ."

"Of course."

She wanted money, she didn't want a roll in the hay. Oh, she might have wanted that, too, if the truth be known. Everything was so damned confusing. She had loved Edward, loved him deeply and fully. But after his death she had discovered that the Edward she had loved had never truly existed. She had loved only a shadow of her imagination.

Edward, she now knew, was not the strong pillar she had imagined. He was not the industrial wizard she and others had erroneously considered him, either. Edward had not managed the mill correctly. He had been, as she now understood, deeply in debt to the bank for loans taken out to continue operation of the textile factory. A third of the workers had been dismissed already, and with no hope of financial improvement for those still employed, others were leaving for work in Charleston or going to North Carolina and even Georgia. Housing in Greenridge had not kept pace with the rest of the country, and decent dwellings, if available, were too expensive to afford on the wages paid by the mill.

Why, Roy Bucks, the very man who had killed Edward, was—as Aggie had pointed out with such relish—a disgruntled worker, crazed by financial pressures for which he'd held Edward personally accountable.

Mason had explained the facts of her salvation to her. The bank was willing to take the mill off Elizabeth's hands. And mind. How loathe everyone was to have thoughts pass through her head! Relinquishing ownership of her own accord would, Mason emphasized during a prior meeting, save her the humiliation of a public foreclosure.

"Mason," Elizabeth said now, crossing the veranda to where he stood, "I don't mean to let the ugliness of business intrude upon what has been a perfectly beautiful evening, but do you think there is any chance of turning the operation of the mill around? With the right management and some additional funding?"

Although his features remained immobile, Mason's eyes seemed to glaze over. "We've gone through this, Elizabeth."

"Yes, I know."

"There's no hope of survival. Things have gone too far. If we close down the factory, sell what inventory of raw stock exists and auction off every last bit of equipment, we're still claiming a terrible loss."

"But if I'm not to get a cent anyway, what would be my benefit of giving up without a fight?" Elizabeth pushed, knowing even as she did that she was going too far in her cerebral exploration of the situation.

"You'd have your pride intact, Elizabeth," Mason responded testily.

"Pride? Pride, Mason? Pride won't feed me."

"I could." He paused, gathered together his words. "We would make a good team, Elizabeth. Your family name, my current position in the community. And more," he said, spontaneous enthusiasm erupting across his usually unexpressive face. "I have plans of a much larger scale than Greenridge. Political plans. Together, you and I, well, we could go as far as the Governor's mansion.''

"You're saying . . . ?"

"Yes."

Elizabeth knew by his tone, by the hard glint of determination behind his eyes, that Mason was serious.

"Could that be a proposal of marriage?"

"Oh, how stupid. Yes, yes, Elizabeth, it is, and forgive me. I hadn't meant it to be like this. The moonlight, yes. But I had meant to be more courtly.'' Flustered, he stopped. Stepping in closer to her, he took up her hand and, holding it in both of his, looked deeply into her eyes and asked, "Will you marry me, Elizabeth?"

"Mason, I—"

"After a respectful period of time has passed, of course!"

At that moment, a sick feeling slid within her soul, contaminating her determination to rescue herself through feminine charm. She gazed at Mason as if he were a painting. Could she really love this man as her husband? Was this right? Was anything right?

"I can't give you an answer now. It's too soon."

"Not an answer, then. Only a promise that you'll consider my offer."

"Yes, of course, of course I'll think about it."

"Elizabeth," Mason said darkly, "it's the only way for you." Elizabeth said nothing. "You'll be able to keep all of this. Everything will go on just as it was before, as it was with Edward. Only I'll be here to take care of you."

And it was at that point, the sickness lifted. She suddenly realized that she did not want things to go on as they were before. Since the day at the fair, when Edward had fallen, a window had opened in her. Perhaps it was only a crack thus far, but nevertheless, the slightest of breezes, bearing the scent of previously unimagined shores, had caressed her. It was likely she might shipwreck herself on rocks before she found herself in a new land, but she realized, standing before the staid and predictable Mason Philips, that she would have to at least set sail. Turning back had never really been an option.

Chapter Four

For the next three days Elizabeth experienced a raging headache from staring at ledgers. At first she had no idea what she was looking at, or even looking for, but after a while the stiff numbers in their neat columns took on the flavor of reading a book filled with colorful history. When she had closed the last profit-and-loss statement, she was certain of one thing: Edward had not had a head for business.

The mill had been in her family for generations, since long before the Civil War. Also in her heritage were four senators, two congressmen, and three governors. No wonder Mason Philips was so intent on their alliance. She would make an enviable talisman when he launched his star.

Never, however, had there been a female in her illustrious genealogy table who had distinguished herself in anything other than smiling. But never had there been a reason to do anything but simper, Elizabeth thought. Now there was. She could only hope that out of a long line of strong-willed male forebears, at least a drop of courage had filtered down into her veins.

On the fourth day she placed an advertisement in the *Wall Street Journal* requesting advice from a management firm. Response was forthcoming, but most of the companies wanted money up front, and those who did agree to look at her books and take a percentage of profits once the mill was out of the red, turned her down. They simply didn't see a turn around as being in the cards. There was, however, one reply that painted a more hopeful picture of the mill's chances for success if managed properly. Elizabeth considered the offer long and hard, and in the end rejected the proposal. The man would agree to manage the mill in return for half interest immediately. She could not turn over her family's enterprise to an outsider.

Instead, she worked as manager herself, and at night, exhausted from the day's bewildering array of battles, studied what books she could on financial management.

She had set sail. And she was floundering.

When it became clear she would have to cut corners further if she were to pay the remaining skeleton work crew at the mill, she made her house available to the state historical society and suffered through busloads of people interested in reliving the flavor of the Old South. For this she received a percentage from the tickets sold, plus a flat monthly fee from the society.

But the tours were seasonal. Winters, although mild, would not draw hoards of tourists.

To fill the financial gap, Elizabeth began renting rooms in the mansion, granting boarders access to the kitchen and other living quarters. In truth, she found the huge empty house oppressive, and although on one level it seemed a deep humiliation to be reduced to such common straits as becoming landlady to strangers, the sense of other bodies in the house made her feel more secure.

But even with all these measures, she was merely bobbing up for gulps of air in the sea of financial debt. That she would soon, and finally, drown was an imminent probability supported in full by each weekly balance sheet.

It was the last weekend of September. A spell of heat had moved into the town several days before. Elizabeth, standing on the front porch in the same spot Mason Philips had occupied during the night of his proposal, watched the steam rise in a mist beyond the blacktop fronting her home. She thought of a dying dragon, bellowing its last breath, in a place where the earth turned to swamp and ancient trees grew dense and drooped with moss. She thought of the mill.

As she stood there, listening to the dim music coming from one of her boarder's radios, a car turned off the roadway into her drive.

It was a dark green late-model sedan with New York plates, and from its appearance had been driven the whole way. Bugs in the front grill and windshield and a heavy film of dust gave evidence of the vehicle's distant origin.

Elizabeth waited with the curiosity of a shut-in, both anticipating with excitement and fearing the consequence of an unexpected visitor. The only surprises she had experienced since Edward's death were not of the positive variety. On the other hand, there was so little that emotionally interested her that even a new jolt of adversity was welcome, if for no other reason than it shocked her system out of its lethargy.

Headlights were shut off, then the engine. From the driver's side, a man appeared.

He stood behind the vehicle's open door for a moment, looking toward the house.

She doubted he could see her. The porch was in shadow, with only the faintest bit of light seeping from the house.

Concealed, it was easier for her to observe him. He was tall and dressed in casual good taste, his frame encased in an unstructured jacket, casual slacks, and what appeared to be a light colored—probably blue—shirt, the neck open to a deep vee. His hair was dark and straight and long enough to look tousled by the wind from an open window. A straight lock had fallen over his forehead, and as he raised his face to search for the source of the music spilling from the house, he brushed the strand aside.

"Hello, out there," Elizabeth called from her shadowy retreat.

The man shifted his gaze, seeking her out.

Elizabeth stepped forward. "Can I help you?"

There was the barest of pauses, then he said, "Yeah, thanks. I'm looking for a room." His voice was a smooth baritone, devoid of regional accent.

"You do know this isn't a hotel, don't you?" Elizabeth asked. "It's for long-term guests. If you're just passing through, you might want to try the Greenridge Inn."

He came forward slowly, like a dark cat, she thought, whose senses took in more than the eyes could see. "I plan to stay a while," he said, pausing just at the base of the steps leading to the porch.

She looked down to where he stood, serenely composed, watching her. There was nothing untoward in his manner, yet under his placid scrutiny she felt herself being efficiently dissected.

Her hair was loose, and she wore a pink cotton dress whose neckline was scooped low, at a point somewhere between modest and provocative. Her boarders had retired early, as was their habit. She had not expected to see any of them the rest of the evening, nor had she anticipated having to welcome a visitor. So an hour before, she had removed the constriction of her strapless bra before coming out on the veranda to greet the night. Fervently, she wished she had not. With every movement she was aware of her body's undulating outline, and the hardened peaks of her nipples were impossible to disguise beneath the fabric that in the heat had molded itself to her form.

"There's only one room available," she said in a discouraging voice. In a vague way, she sensed the man's presence was a dangerous complication in her already complicated existence.

"There's only one of me," the man returned. "What's it like?"

"It's a good room," Elizabeth said. "Larger and more expensive than the others."

"How expensive?" he inquired, apparently undaunted.

Instinct and observation told her that money was not an issue with the man. He did not look like the usual itinerant boarder, someone hovering between good fortune and bad, either on his way up or down the scale of financial solvency, as some of her boarders clearly were.

"The room's fifty dollars a week. If you want any of your meals, that's extra, of course."

"Okay, I'd like to see it."

"And no overnight guests," Elizabeth added.

He smiled at that. "Sounds fair." He waited, with dark eyes glittering in the spill of light from the open screen door. There was a sense of patience borne of certainty that everything would go as he wanted.

"It's upstairs." She turned and he followed her into the large formal foyer, where an impressive staircase wound to the upper story.

There was nothing in his manner that could account for her feelings, yet she continued to find his presence strangely provocative as they climbed the stairs to the second floor. Outside there had been a sense of command about him, and the feeling that she was being shown her own house, rather than the other way around, persisted.

In the light she saw that his eyes were not black as she had originally thought. They were green, a remarkable shade, alive with intelligence and emotions she could not fathom. Like inserts of green glass, they sparkled and grew mysteriously opaque depending on some exercise of his will.

He was six feet and an inch or two more, with dark hair, its coarseness permitting only the slightest wave to exist. His build was lean, but in no way did he appear wan or effete. It was the willowy, masculine form of a born athlete. His smile had appeared only once, when she had mentioned the taboo of overnight guests, but the sample was enough to warn her of its power. The brooding somberness of his expression had dissolved into a radiant glow of masculine charm, and she suspected he knew exactly its effect and could ration it as needed.

A fleeting thought crossed her mind that she—always so certain of the power of her physical attributes—had met her match. This man, moving silently beside her as they ascended the staircase, bore an assuredness that edged on calculation. Secure within himself, he seemed one of those people who could afford to relax and play life as a chess game.

In the room, he moved about silently, inspecting the premises as Elizabeth outlined various features. "So the furniture is really quite rare, everything antique. And valuable," she stressed, hoping to ensure the proper respect for its care if he chose to stay. "This was always used as our principal guest room."

"It's fine. I'll take it," he said, again as if the decision of his board was solely his to make. "And I'll treat your furniture with its due respect," he added gravely, having understood the message.

"Of course I'll need references," Elizabeth said. "Do you have references? Because otherwise I couldn't possibly—"

"Yes, of course." He smiled slightly, as if she had just made another anticipated move on his chess board. "I come complete with a verifiable past. For openers," he said, "my name's Cade Delaney." He paused, as if giving her a chance to refute the information. "I'm sure my credentials will be sufficient." From inside his jacket, he withdrew an envelope and crossed the room to Elizabeth. "Please," he said, inviting her to study the contents.

Elizabeth read quickly. He was from New York City and owned an apartment on Park Avenue. The address and telephone number of the supervisor were listed, along with his own. She didn't know much about New York City, but she knew Park Avenue as being an impressive place to hang one's hat. There was a bank listed with an account number.

"What sort of work do you do?" Elizabeth asked, looking up.

"A little of this and that. I'm an entrepreneur. Afraid my occupation's hard to catalogue neatly. But the bank will vouch for my financial solvency."

"Obviously the 'this' and 'that' has paid dividends."

"A few," he said, offering, as Elizabeth had expected, nothing more in way of information. She realized then how strange it was that the arrogance he exuded was attributable to *not* displaying his worth, rather than boorishly expounding on his merits as most people bent to impress did.

"Don't you think you're a little off the beaten track? Greenridge doesn't seem like it would be your kind of place."

"Oh? Why's that?"

"Well, we're a little outpost in the wilderness, so to speak. In Texas that might be okay because in those little hayseed towns they've got oil and gas and coal. But there's no black gold here. No computer mecca, either. In fact, we don't have anything here but unemployment and country gossip. Oh, yes, and heat. Plenty of heat."

"I'll think of it as an interesting change of pace."

"Ummm, that's another problem. We seem to lack pace here, along with everything else," Elizabeth said dryly. "What we've got is a dead stop."

A heavy, strangely sensual silence fell between them. Only one lamp was on, and in consequence they were cloaked in a fuzzy, surreal glow. It was as if the two of them had been caught between the real world and some other in which the usual rules of life were suspended. If at that moment he had reached across for her and drawn her to him, she knew she could not have stopped him. If he had lowered the thin pieces of material from her bare shoulders and slipped the fabric to her waist, she would have allowed it to happen. If—

"So I'll just get my things," he said. "Oh, and if it's agreeable, I'll settle cash for the first week in advance and write a check for the remainder of the month. The check should clear by next week."

Elizabeth consented.

He was halfway to the door when she suddenly remembered her manners. "Oh, sorry. I never introduced myself. Elizabeth Hart."

Pausing, he glanced sideways and smiled again. "Yeah, I can see it. You look like an Elizabeth. Exactly the way I'd picture an Elizabeth to look."

"Oh? How's that?" she asked, amused and curious.

"Like a lady. Someone cool and pampered and sure of herself and her world."

"Well, I used to look like an Elizabeth," she returned with a light laugh. He waited for her to elaborate, and she did. "But things changed. And so did I."

The green eyes watching her seemed to close in on themselves, becoming darker, even more impenetrable. The man named Cade Delaney passed his gaze from her face to the French doors leading off his bedroom to the outside balcony. "Looks like you could use a little water around here. When did it rain last?" he asked.

"Not for three months, except for some sprinkles not amounting to much. You must have heard, everyone has. It's been in all the news reports. A state emergency. A crisis."

"Then I'd say the worst is yet to come," he said. "When it finally does open up, all hell's going to break loose. Parched land runs wild." A faint smile accompanied his statement, and with a final look, devoid of emotion, he departed for his things.

Elizabeth left him a typed sheet of rules and placed bath towels on his bed. She looked down at the coverlet and a surge of heat traveled through her body as she envisioned him lying there. *Parched land, turning into a wild river when the rains come.* He hadn't been talking about the weather or the land. It was her he had meant. Somehow he'd felt it, felt her aridness. Humiliation swept over her, and she told herself she was only imagining things. It was the heat. The heat was to blame for a great many things.

Outside, the car door slammed.

She left the door to his room open and went to her own, next door. A minute later she listened to the new boarder's footsteps on the stairs. She was already undressed, her nightgown dangling in her hand. The barest breeze stirred, and its caress against her body made her shiver as if fingers had touched her skin.

Across the room, in the mirror of her vanity, she made out the diffused ghostly form of her nude body and stared at herself, fascinated, as if through a stranger's eyes. She was still a beautiful woman.

In the adjoining room she heard faint movements: a drawer opening, footsteps, the scrape of a chair, the closet door shutting. She imagined him on the other side of the wall, and wondered what thoughts he had as he went about his routine chores of settling in to a new environment. Did he have a woman somewhere? She remembered the slow, insinuating and finally dazzling smile of the man. The lips were...they curved gently, not full, not thin. Yes, of course, he would have a woman. Most likely he would have several and his heart would belong to none of them.

Although life in Greenridge did not foster a particularly worldly outlook, she had nevertheless determined that men who made a great show of themselves were not generally those who were the most romantically experienced. For this reason she suspected her boarder was of the opposite variety. In his quiet, assured way, he would easily steal a heart or two or ten.

Next door the shower went on. She imagined him standing wet beneath the stream of water, head thrown back, black hair sleek. His body would be hard and muscular. A yearning rose within her like an ache. It had been months since she had experienced physical desire. In contrast, for years lovemaking had been a daily satisfaction for her. Remembrance of that part of her life was, like everything else, a distant echo in her consciousness.

She slipped the gown on and put out the lights, lying for some time in the dark with thoughts circling crazily. There was no purpose or content to any of them. Agitated, she turned to her side, then shifted directions, lay on her back, and finally rose and sought the cool of her balcony.

The gown's filmy material clung damply to her body, and when she moved the pressure of the material over her breasts and the hug of silk against her thighs only reminded and increased the longing for a man's touch.

Cade also could not sleep. On the desk in his room was the folder he had unpacked. He studied it again, for the hundredth time. The advertisement run by Elizabeth in the *Wall Street Journal* was there, along with the mill's financial statement, sent to him when he replied as a management consultant.

She had turned down his offer to take over running the company for half interest, but the temptation to at last satisfy the debt owed his father had won over his revulsion and fear of returning to Greenridge. His father had lost, but this time the son would triumph. That was his vision. That was the way he saw it.

Barefoot, without a shirt, he sat at the desk in a pair of light linen slacks, feeling the day's heat still burning through the night. He recalled other summers when the rains had not come in Greenridge. Across town from the Huntington mansion, he had lain awake in his family's little shack of a place, the air close and heavy on his lungs. He had thought of Elizabeth then, as he did now, wondering if she lay cool in a large room, in a large bed, atop silken sheets as smooth to the touch as her skin.

In the silence, he heard a slight stirring.

He stepped quietly to his French doors to investigate. Hidden in the shadows, he saw Elizabeth not twenty feet beyond, her figure faint in the moonlight. A soft sheath of fabric, silvery and luminous, covered her. He could make out the curve of full, high breasts, the flare of hips and buttocks, the taper of slender legs.

Aroused, he stepped farther back, afraid she might notice his presence. For a while, he remained in the shadows, his own flesh burning as he watched her.

Love, hate, unadulterated lust swirled within him, each emotion chasing the tail of the last.

Then she stepped away, dissolving into her room and out of view.

That night as he stared into the dark, he knew with an absolute certainty he would have the mill. And he would have her. He would take both, any way he had to, but take them he would. It would not be long before he would have his victory.

Chapter Five

A week had passed since Cade Delaney had arrived on the premises. Although the three other boarders had added a sense of life to the hollowness of the house, Elizabeth's general sense of detachment and disinterest in the world had for the most part persisted. But now, with the addition of only one man, the atmosphere had mysteriously altered. His presence generated a sense of expectancy. For what, Elizabeth had no idea, yet she was forced to acknowledge the feeling that dominated large blocks of her day.

Oddly, she rarely saw him. More often than not he would leave early and return late in the evening. Even so, as the days progressed, her fascination with her aloof boarder grew in direct proportion to the paucity of their contact.

She even began to listen consciously for the sound of his car leaving or returning. If she was in the kitchen and the front door closed, her heart would stop and all her senses would focus on the cadence of footsteps passing from the entry to the stairs. Within two days she had memorized the particular rhythm of his walk, which was soft and even, not shuffling or erratic or stealthy as were those of the others who shared her roof.

If it was very late she would lie awake and wait for him to return. At the sharp click of his bedroom door, she would hold her breath, ears straining to catch some added clue to his personal situation. Everything about him was an enigma.

But the mystery she yearned to solve persisted, and even after a week there was little to be pieced together from observation. She knew he showered at night, and he rose early, even before she had put coffee for the lodgers on the dining room sideboard. Then he went somewhere. But where? And why? The unanswered questions tantalized, invaded her every waking space as she continued to spin fantasies around him.

Twice one day she passed him on the stairs. Each time he was dressed casually, in faded jeans and blue work shirt and serviceable boots. There was a coating of dust over the boots and remnants of mud clods attached to the soles, which she noted he considerately took time to clean before entering the house.

Once, Elizabeth thought, this man had been a boy somewhere, some mother's son who had been taught manners, who had been rocked to sleep as a baby, who had cuts bandaged when he fell as a toddler. Thinking of him in these terms made him more human. It served to bring him down to a more manageable human scale.

"Hello," he had said, when their paths had converged on the stairway.

"Hello," she returned with nonchalance. Then, as he'd begun to withdraw, she had become desperate. "Did you see it outside? The sky? It may rain!"

Looking sideways, he seemed to consider her rather than what she had proposed for the elements. "No, not yet," he answered. There was a pause, and he said, "But it will. Eventually."

In the diffused light of the stairwell, his eyes were as dark as obsidian. Like arrows, hard as the stone, he seemed to take aim at her soul with his gaze. When he left, she felt violated, as if she had been taken by force and left used and alone on some rocky shore. The grip of his look stayed with her for some hours after that brief interchange.

The erotic intrigue he generated in her life came more and more to overwhelm the usual daily concerns. Even the urgency of rescuing the mill and the specter of her imminent financial insolvency would often dim in importance. She began to harbor the wild notion that something beyond herself had taken control; that through some alchemy of Cade Delaney's manufacture, she would eventually lose herself entirely.

And she didn't care. That was the ridiculous part of it!

For the danger she sensed in his presence brought with it an addictive thrill. She would have gladly sacrificed herself rather than forfeit the excitement that had replaced the stagnancy of her life.

But nothing actually happened. The play was all in her mind.

The footsteps on the stairs, the sound of the shower next to her room being turned on, turned off, the brief non-conversations in passing—these were the sole elements constituting her relationship with her magnetic boarder.

Then, on the seventh morning of his stay she found an envelope with a personal check left for her on the dining table. It was meant to cover the remainder of the month.

The check was in her hand when she suddenly became aware of being watched. Looking up, she found Cade at the entrance to the dining room.

"I thought I should tell you . . ." he began.

"Yes, I know. It's for the rest of the month. That's fine."

"But there's a chance I might be leaving. Before the month's over. If it happens, naturally I expect you to keep the total amount of the rent."

"Yes, I see. Of course." She stared at the check, trying to hide her disappointment.

"And I'm sorry if it would put you out in any way." His voice was a soft velvety purr, the eyes, as always, holding that same unexplainable intensity of expression, as if he were engaged in some passionate, all-consuming enterprise known only to him.

Elizabeth feigned a nonchalance she didn't feel. "Really, we're only a hotel here. All of this may give the appearance of stability, but people come and go just the same." She laughed.

Beneath the facade of light humor, her heart felt as if it had been raked over by a sharp hoe. At the thought of Cade's departure, she experienced that sense of dying again, just as she had when the reality of Edward's death had taken hold. The idea that the illusive magic would be withdrawn from her life, that her days would again dwindle to their dry sameness, filled her with a crippling disappointment.

"Good. Then I'm glad there won't be any problem." He seemed about to leave.

In that instant, before he could start away, Elizabeth suddenly asked, "You never mentioned what brought you to Greenridge?"

From across the room, she felt him tense, and he sent her what she interpreted as a searing look of reproval for trying to cross his personal boundaries. But when he spoke there was no particular emotion in his voice, and she had to conclude that she had again been a victim of her fertile, runaway imagination.

"Just some old business," he answered simply.

"Really? Old business, you say? Meaning that you were here before?" This interested her. Enough so that the hold his physical presence had over her was momentarily neutralized, and her focus kept to the subject at hand.

"Let's call it passing through. It was a long time ago," he qualified.

"Hmm..." she said, considering. "I'm surprised."

"How's that?"

He seemed suddenly as interested in her response as she was in his story.

Actually, she enjoyed the unexpected engagement of intellect. It gave a sense of form to a relationship that had seemed unreal. "It's just that Greenridge isn't the kind of place people pass through," she completed, adopting his terminology.

"No? What sort of place is your town then?"

For a moment she was struck by the strange note of coldness in his voice, but she pushed it aside as a sardonic thought of her own came to mind, and she smiled. "You've been here for a week. I should think you'd know the answer to that by now. It doesn't take long to get the lay of the land in these parts."

"True," he agreed, again congenial. "But maybe I'd like to hear your version."

Elizabeth thought, hunting for a concise response. "It's just a place where dust settles."

"People live and grow old and die, that sort of place," he elaborated.

"Something like that, yes. Exactly like that."

"And nothing else ever happens?"

"Happens? Sure," she agreed with a laugh. "Sometimes the dust gets swept away." She slapped the envelope containing his check onto the table, as if the action punctuated a pronouncement of fate. "What else could there be in Greenridge?"

"I don't know." He looked past her to the window, and she could tell by his stare that his mind was on some other world, or some other time. "I suppose I would have imagined a world of secret passions," he murmured. "You know...hatreds fermenting, quests of various kinds being undertaken. Moral, financial..."

Elizabeth shook her head. "Sorry, I'm afraid you find that only in novels. And movies. Paul Newman always plays the lead. The reality here is the dust in the summer, the mud in the winter. Passion is when a neighbor's dog digs up your prize rose bush and you get angry enough to yell something hostile at its owner. Maybe you don't speak for three weeks. There's your seething Greenridge passion." She paused. "So old business brought you back. What kind?"

"The kind that went unfinished."

"I see," Elizabeth replied. "And apparently that kind is classified information?"

"For the time being," he said agreeably.

"You're a very mysterious man, Mr. Delaney."

"Sometimes it's the only way."

"Yes." Elizabeth considered. "Well, there's something about fishing in deep water that's very compelling. But it's not polite, is it, to fish in someone else's pond? I was brought up to be polite," Elizabeth said dryly. "Therefore, I apologize for any ripples I may have caused." She said it good-naturedly, yet she felt slightly defeated, as if she had made it almost to the finish line with the ball and then fumbled.

"No problem," Cade said easily. "I was brought up to handle trespassers."

"Once a man came to Greenridge. He stayed three days at the hotel in town. He didn't talk to anyone. He took some long walks. One night he shot himself in his room."

"Why?" he asked.

"No one ever knew," Elizabeth said blandly, her point wrapped in the delivery. But in case he had missed it, she added, "I doubt that anyone much cared. And that, Mr. Delaney, sums up Greenridge."

"I promise not to shoot myself in my room. I'd hate my death to go unmourned."

"Good. There are better places to die. Besides, the sight of blood is not my favorite picture." That perfect summer's day of weeks before flashed before her in all its sensory fullness. She gripped the table with both hands. Weaving, she tried to draw herself away from the replay of curling golden wood chips and the stain of blood against light blue fabric.

"Elizabeth...Elizabeth...what's happened...are you all right?"

A man's voice was coming to her through a tunnel. "What?" Elizabeth's eyes refocused. Cade was at her side, supporting her, and only then did she realize that her legs had buckled from under her. Strength returned gradually, along with the fuzzy awareness of her environment. "Thanks," she said finally. "I think I've got it together now." He lessened the pressure of his grip, but remained where he was.

"You almost fell," he said. His concern sounded cool, as if he were being polite but did not want to become involved. "You're not ill?"

They were standing close, dangerously so by Elizabeth's way of thinking. The flow of his breath brushed against her neck, and a different kind of panic assailed her. It was born of a desire so fierce she thought she might actually crush herself against him in an agony of sexual longing. "I'm all right now." She began to draw away, but he held her back with one hand still firmly attached to her arm. She was acutely aware of the physical connection. The focus of her entire being seemed centered at the single point where their bodies were joined.

"Maybe you should rest," he suggested.

"No. I can't. There's too much to do."

He retained his hold on her, and she wondered at that. She felt there was nothing left of her solid enough to grasp; her body had dissolved into a river of sensual longing.

"Come on, I'll see you up to your room. You really ought to rest."

"It's not necessary. Honestly," she protested. "I'll be okay. And I do really have a million things waiting to get done." She looked into the blank screen of his eyes. If there was concern or pity or lust to match her own behind the green wall, she couldn't tell. He was obviously in perfect control while she fell apart before him.

"Okay, a million things . . . then consider this as the first of them," he said, and somehow, in a waking dream, she was being led up the stairs. The journey seemed to take forever. Or maybe it took no time at all. Who could tell? Nothing was real anymore; there were no familiar emotional landmarks to grip and stabilize herself as long as she was in his company.

He pushed open the bedroom door as if he had done so a thousand times. And a fleeting thought brought forth to Elizabeth what seemed a ridiculous truth, but a truth nonetheless: from the moment he had arrived on that first night, Cade Delaney had owned her. He had taken possession of this home, as well. And now she knew that somehow, in the subtle act of crossing over this threshold, she would be formally relinquishing to him all of her rights forever.

Frantic, Elizabeth turned. It was the place and time for a stand. "Thank you," she said. "I'll rest . . . thank you . . ."

"I'll see you get settled in." The look on his face was adamant and washed away whatever feeble noise of protest she had been about to make.

The threshold was crossed.

"Really, I'll be fine," she said turning, shocked to find the man she had fantasized over so many nights in the very factory of those heated dreams.

It was disconcerting, but there was also an inevitability to the scene. It was almost as if in hindsight she could follow the threads of the past leading to this single moment. There had been the first night, when they had met—her lonely vigil on the porch, waiting secretly for something or someone to fill the empty well of her life. Perhaps out of her extreme longing she had drawn him from the dark into her existence. There was, in fact, that shadowed, insubstantial quality about him, as if he might actually have been fashioned out of nocturnal fantasies. Perhaps he did not exist except in her mind. Or perhaps he existed as a real entity in another dimension, and came forth only when summoned by the imaginations of women. He had that kind of power about him.

While she watched, he drew the covers off her bed. The pink silk sheets shone in the soft light coming through the white nylon sheers she had drawn across the French doors opening onto the balcony. There was a small breeze, and the cloth billowed out like a ship's sails.

In the filtered light, his skin appeared tawny and golden and smooth, a man polished to a satin finish. And beyond the outer man, was an inner one, whom she suddenly glimpsed, so acutely tuned were her senses. She saw that he had no rough edges internally, either. He was a man who could slip easily through life, his soul never collecting the snags other people drew into their lives.

For a time, like figures in a dream, they continued to exchange mundane conversation, layers of unspoken feelings disguised in trivia.

"Thank you," she said, at last seated at the edge of the bed. "Maybe I should rest. You're probably right. Maybe I needed to put it all aside."

He smiled slightly, and saying nothing, moved to the door. She followed him with her eyes. There was a moment's hesitation, as if he weighed something, then he closed the door and secured the lock.

When he turned back to her, he swept her with a look of assured possession.

"No," she said, but made no physical move that would lend credence to her refusal. "I'm afraid you've misunderstood."

"No," he said. "I've not misunderstood."

He moved forward, emerald eyes fixed on her face, burning his intention into her as if the act of exercising his mental will over her was more important than the deed of taking her physically.

"But you have, you see . . . okay, yes . . . I admit I've found you attractive. I'm sorry if I've . . . please," she said and tried to finish, but his nearness thrilled her, and filled her with a desire she was unable to banish.

"Take off your dress, Elizabeth."

Slowly, mesmerized, her fingers went to her top button, but held, unmoving there. "I don't know if I can." Her voice was warm, fluid, and she could not remove her eyes from his hands.

"Go on," he whispered. "You're a woman, you're not a schoolgirl. You know you want this to happen. I've wanted you, you've wanted me. And now . . ."

"I haven't done anything like this before," she said in a low voice, and it was the truth. Suddenly, she seemed ashamed that it was. Her sexual life with Edward had been almost polite, in terms of the raw sensuality Cade promised.

Cade stared at her for a moment, disbelief washing across his face, followed by what she read as disappointment—for her? for him?—and then he said with an odd smile, "Well, then, it's time you became educated to the ways of the real world, my lovely Elizabeth."

Again, she thought, that phrase—the real world. Aggie had said it, too. *The real world.*

"How long?" he asked conversationally, as if they were talking of the weather again. "How long has it been since you've been with a man?" By now his shoes were discarded.

"My husband died," she said in a mumble, her eyes lowered. "Did you know that?"

"I knew, yes."

"Yes, everyone knows." She sighed, wondering if everyone would someday know about this as well. "I haven't been with anyone. Not for a long time. Not since Edward." It was the first time she had mentioned her husband's name to Cade. It seemed at once a breach of something holy, but it also bore with it a sense of abandon that was freeing. Briefly, a part of her spirit soared, as if she had dared to execute wonderful loops in the sky and had not been shot down for her bravery.

He flung the blue work shirt to the side. In the silence, it dropped heavily to the floor. The sound of a gavel.

Her eyes affixed themselves to the shirt, afraid, yet wanting to look directly at him. But she couldn't. She was too ashamed of her desire.

Next, she heard the jean fabric slip to the floor, and from the corner of her eye saw that he was stepping free of the denim. A deliberate kick sent the pants flying to join the shirt and shoes.

It was completely still. Only the sheer curtains whispered. She could sense his amusement as he waited for her reaction.

Trembling, she raised her eyes slowly to his nude form.

He smiled. "Now you."

She hesitated, her heart pumping madly. Longing filled her with a wildness that she had never before experienced. The long slow tease in the golden light was something beyond her ken. All those years with Edward and she had never, never known this racing, this rush of energy that was spinning her out of control.

Shaken, almost helpless with desire, she looked into his eyes. Two dark burning mirrors reflected nothing of the man within, and his very denial of entrance past that outer gate made her his captive. She wanted to know him, she had to get past the closed entrance to experience what lay within.

His body was magnificent. Partially aroused, but still in control, promising, but not yet willing to deliver, he stood before her with natural, unashamed grace. He might have been a statue of the highest artistic order. She thought also of a sleek cat, a panther, an animal that was dangerous and cruel and expert, from which there would be no false moves. To die in the grip of such a beast was to lose one's life to a master killer.

"Elizabeth?"

Her fingers released the first button.

He waited, watching her, until the row of pale ivory was undone.

"Stand up," he said softly.

"What?" She was so nervous, she couldn't hear, couldn't think.

"Stand up."

Slowly, the dream state persisting, she stood up.

"Now," he said, "open the top of your dress."

She hesitated. Despite all she felt, all she wanted, she couldn't do it. She lifted her face, her eyes pleading with him to understand.

He stared back at her. Time seemed suspended as he waited for her to make a decision. He wasn't the one who needed to choose. She had to do it. But she could only look at him.

"Okay. Never mind," he said. "Fasten your dress. Lock your life back up. Save yourself for...whatever." He made a move to gather up his things.

"No, wait." Closing her eyes, she drew in a breath and let the material fall away from her bare breasts.

Her nipples hardened, and she felt as if his fingers, rather than his eyes, played against their peaks. Shame of her weakness, and desire for union with him, moved in through her in ever tightening circles.

"Please..." she said. "I don't know how..."

"Yes you do. It's instinctive. It's part of life. So live..." Cade ordered, and she heard an urgency behind the command that had not been there before.

Haltingly, she stepped out of the dress and stood before him. Slowly, she opened her eyes and defiantly now, faced him fully.

Slowly he approached her, his eyes never wavering as with one hand he cupped and fondled a breast. She closed her eyes, melting from the heat welling up within her, as forefinger and thumb teased the peak.

"Open your eyes..." he said in a low voice. "I want to see into your eyes, straight into your soul..."

With his other hand, he drifted lower, his touch like liquid fire across her belly, and below, he found the soft apex. She moaned and again closed her eyes from the ecstasy coursing through her loins.

He transferred her hand to his body, and positioned her fingers against him. "Oh, God..." Elizabeth whispered. She was on fire, the heat consuming her, driving her mad.

He kissed her then, a demanding kiss that she couldn't deny, that she could only equal with her responses. She didn't protest when Cade led her to the bed. He was hard against her, still he didn't take her, although now she had the satisfaction of hearing the ragged edge to his breathing and seeing a light in his eyes that flickered, no longer steady and in control.

"This is going to be very real," he said, looking down into her eyes. "You are going to feel this morning for the rest of your life. You are going to taste this morning for every day you remain on this earth. You are going to go places with me you never dreamed existed. It's all going to happen on this bed, now."

Chapter Six

Cade proved his words in ways she had never imagined.

"How do you know all of this?" she murmured, as he traveled down the length of her body, his tongue a liquid ember against her skin. "Where did you learn?"

"Arch, lift . . ." he said, and she obeyed him, curious and needful and apprehensive.

The letting go was difficult for her. The exquisite sensations forced her to reject years of her life with Edward, who now, in her fleeting thoughts, appeared in contrast as a bumbling, selfish lover. This had been available always, and she had never known.

Then all thought faded as Cade pressed his mouth against her and suddenly no instructions were necessary. One did not need to be taught these things; they happened naturally. Under the right circumstances. With the right person. Her hips moved in a rhythm that was automatic, spiraling to an inner music that sent a vibration singing through her soul.

Ragged and uncontrolled, her breath seemed to lead her from level to level of pleasure, until a soft scream filled the room's silence and her body rose again and again as tremors passed through her, expanding, contracting. She flew through universes having no boundaries and drifted on wave after wave of pleasure in oceans without shores.

Cade was with her, guiding her, his presence never forgotten, but the sensations fully her own to experience.

Her body was drenched in sweat, as was his. Her hands slid against his skin and fingers twined in the thatch of black hair, so wet now that he might have just stepped from the shower into her arms.

"I've never known this," she said, and a tear followed her words.

"I know," he said softly. "I know..." And these two words were somewhat sadder in inflection.

He brought himself up to her and looked for a long moment into her eyes, then closed his own and bent to kiss her with a sensitivity he had not shown before. "Elizabeth...my beautiful, foolish Elizabeth," he whispered tenderly.

"Why?" she asked. "Why foolish?"

There was a long silence. He turned his face to the side, avoiding her. Finally, he said, "You trust too much."

They were a dark four words, but before she could fully contemplate their meaning, his tongue had sought hers again, and whatever thoughts she had, dissolved in the new torrent of passion.

"You're a good student," he said, just short of a moan.

"An excellent teacher," she replied, unable to say more.

It was true, what he had said. She had not been a woman before this day. Until Cade, she had not been fully alive. But now she was complete, and never, no matter what happened in the future, could anyone or anything take away the certainty of knowing what power existed within her body and soul.

She brought him into her, rising to meet him, and slipping against his body as he entered.

This was union; this was the final merging; this was everything, she thought, as her body became one with his.

She had not considered what would happen after.

And what did happen, was precisely... nothing.

They had fallen into a satiated slumber, the two of them entwined, still pulsing with the ebbing sexual energy of their bodies. No, not only their bodies—there had been something else between them, Elizabeth knew as she drifted into the world of dreams. There had been something more that had united in that final ecstasy they had shared. But what? Could one call it love? No, for they did not know each other. Yet, she felt as if they had always been together, and in some way had been waiting for each other for eternities on end. And finally, she thought—her last thought that morning—they had found each other.

But when she awoke, he was gone.

It was three o'clock in the afternoon. Footsteps on the stairs had broken into her dead sleep, and her first thought was that it was Cade returning to her. Already she missed him! Craved him—not only for his body, but for the sound of his voice. She longed to gaze upon his face, which might, one moment, show intense passion, and the next present to the world a cold, implacable reserve. God only knew the private thoughts he hid behind the depthless green eyes.

But it was not Cade who ascended the stairs. By the sound of the shuffle—halt, scrape, halt, unsure of his step as he was of himself—Elizabeth recognized the gait as belonging to her self-effacing boarder, Mr. Ruckshaw. It was difficult to stem her disappointment.

She consoled herself by luxuriating in memories of the morning's lovemaking. When that became more unbearable than soothing, she left the bed, bathed, powdered and perfumed herself, then dressed in what she felt was her most provocatively alluring dress—red and low cut, with the slightest slit up the side. She had worn it only once, and Edward had looked askance at her the entire evening, as if she were a trollop out to seduce the entire male population of the country club.

Edward. His face wavered before her, as she brushed her hair. *Edward.* Who had he been?

He had been her husband, and she had thought she had loved him. But she hadn't.

The moment the uncharitable thought passed through her mind—even though it was true—she tried to banish it. But she couldn't. The truth screamed in a voice too loud and clear to be silenced.

Edward, her beloved Edward, was just a phony.

Why, oh why, did she not see it sooner?

It was all so clear. He had taken the mill over when he had married her. It was her family's mill, had been for generations. It was the most successful mill in the entire state, and one of the top producing mills in the entire country. And Edward had gotten it when he had gotten her, and he had run it into the ground, all the while pretending to be in such fantastic control.

Control. That was the whole point of Edward's life. There had never been any true joy. Instead, there had been the rigid propriety of their lives.

And now, on top of it all, she knew he had been a selfish, cold lover, who perhaps had merely gotten tired of pretending, those months he had kept away from her.

Thanks to Cade Delaney, she now knew the truth of that.

Like everything else, Edward's interest in her was actually self-interest. If she looked good, he looked good. But she had to be proper, and if she ever had a renegade thought of her own, it had been instantly imprisoned in stern admonishments related to her social position and class status.

Things were going to be different now. She had Cade to thank for opening her eyes. And, leaving her room, she went in search of him, to do just that.

Only he was not in his room; he was nowhere else to be found, either.

After dinner, she waited up for him. Every time a car would pass down the lonely road fronting the house, her heart would leap. Greetings and posings would form in her mind, as she imagined them coming face to face again. But he did not appear.

It was after twelve when she turned off the living room lights and retreated to her room to wait and listen.

He did not return until the early morning. In fact, it was almost dawn when his car made its approach down the long drive.

Burning with fury and passion and shame, Elizabeth listened as the motor stopped and the car door closed.

She wanted to hit him. How she hated him for doing this to her! She felt positively possessed.

She crossed her room as she heard his footsteps take the stairs up from the ground floor. Burning within, she lay her face flat against the wood of her door, hoping, as her heart pounded, that he would stop, rap lightly, and come to her again. She wanted him! How could he not want her just as madly?

The Greenridge Inn was, in appearance, reserved Southern elegance. Yet within its confines, various levels of social interaction existed. Affairs of a carnal nature were consummated and ended. Alliances of other types, from business to innocently social, were formed in the dark bar. Although it was a country inn, it was reasonably large, and what outside commercial traffic there was, ended up there for a good dinner and a good sleep. These shifting, transient faces brought a certain flavor of anonymity to the inn. The owner, a rare transplant from Chicago, kept his secrets to himself and advised the staff to do likewise, although talk went on, regardless.

Cade had entered the bar of the inn shortly after five o'clock. He had spent some time just walking by himself in the country, during which time his thoughts had been muddled, and he had tried to regain the clarity of purpose that had brought him back to Greenridge. All to no avail.

All his well-constructed emotional barriers, his ignoble and clever and treacherous schemes, had crumbled that morning in the bed of the woman he had meant to destroy.

He could not go back into that house until he had regained his sense of control and purpose.

"A double Scotch," he said, taking a bar stool. The room was dark. The paneling was covered with mirrors and wooden ducks and a mounted deer's head and various paintings depicting pastoral scenes. A number of other people had already arrived, some sitting at tables, and others nursing drinks at the bar.

A woman came up to him shortly after he was into his second double.

"Hi," she said, the word a long flow of honey.

"Hi," he said, looking her over, and trying to get a fix on her scam. She was well built and pretty, about thirty, and by dress and accent not from the area.

A few minutes later she had delivered a good portion of her life's story, which was boring and predictable. She also wanted to sleep with him.

When she had made the suggestion, Cade had lowered his eyes and tried not to smile. But it was hard, and when she appeared insulted, he told her he was married and that it wouldn't be right. But he would like to take her for dinner, anyway, as he very much enjoyed her conversation.

That was, perhaps, the biggest lie. But he didn't want to be alone with his thoughts of Elizabeth, and the woman would at least be enough of a diversion to provide some immediate, if temporary relief. It was a momentary stay of execution.

While they dined, Cade watched as people came and went, and tried to remember the faces he had known as a boy. Some were easy to spot, but others were either new arrivals to Greenridge or had changed considerably, as he also had, since they had been young.

Cade, himself, had been thin and his face severely angular. He had grown into it sometime between his twentieth and twenty-second year. His hair had also become darker, and he had gained about three inches from the time he had last set foot as a teenager in Greenridge. He doubted if anyone would recognize him; looking at his own pictures, he was hard pressed to identify the lanky boy with the man he had become. His name then had been Chandon, not Cade. Cade was only a name his mother used.

This was the gamble he had taken, of course, in returning to Greenridge—that he could move anonymously within the community without being suspect. With Elizabeth it was particularly important that he remain an unknown entity, but he doubted very much, very much indeed, that she would ever have attached him to the past they had once shared in the same town.

She had never, to his knowledge, even passed her amazingly large blue eyes over his face then. She had been a princess and he a lowly toad.

Thinking of it that way, as he did now, brought back enough of the bitterness that he could relax somewhat. Yes, he told himself, he must remember, must *force* himself to recall what it had been like. Their encounter hadn't been real; it had merely been an aberration of emotion, and he had created it for a purpose. God help him! He had waited too long to fall into a pit of his own digging.

A man was watching him. He was with two others who were absorbed in conversation. However this third man kept stealing surreptitious glances in Cade's direction.

Who the hell was the guy? Cade ran through faces from his past in Greenridge. Then, hearing one of the men call the name, he remembered. Mason Philips. A clever little bastard whom Cade had always particularly disliked, one of his main persecutors. The guy had been a social-climbing snake, and one of the ways people like Mason elevated themselves was by pushing others down. Cade had definitely been one of the others.

Cade's female partner was now feeling the half bottle of wine she had consumed with her meal. She was giggling and her scooped neckline was even lower than when they had first met.

"I think you've had enough, sweetheart," Cade cautioned, as she went to pour herself another glass from the bottle.

"Oh, pshaw," she gurgled, and began to tip over in her chair.

"I really didn't need this tonight," he muttered, as he quickly leapt from his chair and saved her from a certain sprawl on the carpet. She giggled some more.

Eyes were on them as he lifted her to her feet. His mind instantly flew to Elizabeth, whom he had also saved from falling earlier that day. In that case, his body had been turned to a tongue of fire, feeling her heat, feeling her skin . . . he had never wanted a woman as much as he had wanted Elizabeth that morning . . . and all of his life.

"Come on," he said. "I'm taking you up to your room. What's the number?"

"Hmmm?" Her eyes had gone glassy on him. With a lurch, she had suddenly pressed herself into him, and her mouth was open and wide, tongue thrusting into his, as she pressed herself against him.

Cade was rarely embarrassed. The situation at hand, however, was just short of farce, and he resented having been made the straight man. The other men were virtually leering, and one observer even winked his approval of what he assumed would be Cade's next move, up the stairs and straight into the woman's bed.

Instead, he surprised them.

"Excuse me," he said, to the waiter, just passing. "Call the manager. Tell him one of his guests needs tucking in."

The manager scurried in within the minute, and Cade was relieved of his charge, much to the disappointment of his male audience.

The man Cade had recognized as Mason Philips rose suddenly. "Sir," he called. "Sir, if you have a moment..."

Cade turned partially around, acknowledging Philips with an impartial nod, but nothing more.

Mason came around the table, stood before Cade and, drawing back his head just a bit, took all of Cade in, as if he were examining a horse for purchase. "I know you. I know you, do I not?"

"Mistaken identity," Cade said blandly. "Happens all the time."

"No, I'm sure of it. But from where?"

"I'm from New York. You in the city a lot?"

Mason's mind drew in on itself, as he continued to hunt for the recognition factor. "Nope...nope. You've got family living in these parts?"

"No."

"Well, I see. Sorry, then. Just looked so familiar, I had to ask."

"No problem," Cade said.

"You staying on here?"

"In the Inn? No."

"Greenridge, then?"

"For a time."

"Well, that's mighty fine. We like new faces in town. Spices things up for us. Come on by and play a little cards with us some time. Every Wednesday, here, second floor. We take one of the rooms, smoke it up a bit, have a supply of bourbon and branch on hand. Name's Philips, Mason Philips." He extended his hand.

Reluctantly Cade took the hand, dry as snakeskin. "I'll keep it in mind." Cade began to move on.

"Say, did I get your name?"

"Delaney. Cade."

"Well, Mr. Delaney, we want to welcome you to Greenridge. And hope you enjoy your stay here. Where did you say you're staying?"

"I didn't." He resented the inquisition, and didn't have to put up with it. He was no longer the poor white trash he had once been considered in Greenridge. But it would not suit his purposes if he were to expose himself as the enemy prematurely. "I'm staying in a private home."

Philips furrowed his brow, as a thought obviously crossed his mind. "That wouldn't be the home of Mrs. Edward Hart, would it?"

"The very place," Cade returned, finding it interesting that Philips used Elizabeth's name in conjunction with her deceased husband's. Then he realized why. Philips was warning him off with a subtle reminder that no matter who he thought he was, Elizabeth was a proper woman, and out of his reach. Cade had to smile at that. If Philips only knew. And then it dawned on him that Philips might have his own proprietary interest in Elizabeth. Well, well, he thought. Things could become even more interesting.

"We'll be looking for you, Mr. Delaney."

Cade tipped a finger to his forehead, offering a lazy salute to the three good ol' boys eyeing him with open, jovial country good humor. Faces that signified one thing to Cade: deception. They no more trusted him than he was worth trusting. Only they didn't know it yet. They merely suspected. He felt that, too.

Times have changed, gentlemen. Times—and I—have changed since the old days. So make your best moves. This time, I'll be ready for you.

A moment later he got into his car feeling a lot better. The old hate was back in place. Like a sleeping green serpent, it lay in a tight coil at the base of his gut. It had innumerable heads, one for each and every injustice perpetrated by the reigning powers of Greenridge thirteen years before. He would cultivate it, nurture it, feed it until it was a large snarling beast that could tear the soul out from the town that had victimized his father and the other men brave enough and foolish enough to have stood up for what they had believed to be right.

It was important that he not return to the Hart mansion just yet. Clearly, Elizabeth had scored a victory over him that evening when he had not followed the woman to her hotel room. He was honest enough to admit that and smart enough to know that he would not be able to resist a similar invitation from Elizabeth if he were to return prematurely. It had taken him thirteen years to get to this point. He could not throw it all away now for the pleasures of a woman's body. He could not afford to relinquish his control.

While it was still light, he took a drive to the Hart mill—or the old Huntington mill, as it had previously been known to him. Going there would remind him that he was there to effect a cure long overdue.

The factory was closed down for the day. The eerie quiet of the site matched perfectly the ghostly images unfolding in his mind. Wraiths in blue factory-issued coveralls filed resolutely out from the past, and Cade counted the faces of good men who had protested for better wages and, when they could not get that, voted for unionization alongside his father. He saw his father as he had been, a peaceful man forced to go against his nature to defend what he knew was right. Only wrong had triumphed.

A portion of the original factory still remained, although additions were periodically affixed to the core edifice. This was of brick, two stories, and ranged some fifty feet in width and a hundred and fifty feet long. It had been built in 1835 and did its first commercial service in cotton manufacturing. Historical record had it that slaves belonging to Crawford Huntington had labored for over two years to complete the structure. Years later, the sons of these slaves worked to manufacture blankets for the Confederate Army.

Cade walked through the grounds, seeing everything that had transpired through the filter of time. Along one side, the original stream still ran, and out of Southern sentimentality the first waterwheel had been preserved for posterity. At one time the wheel had operated a saw mill and a corn mill belonging to the Huntingtons, along with the Woolen Cotton carding for carding wool, a cotton gin and textile mill. At the turn of the century a steam engine fueled by wood was added and ran in conjunction with the waterwheel. Industrialization took hold, but the past was never entirely lost. Even today it clung to the town's atmosphere.

There was such peace, such amazing tranquility to the surroundings. Cade moved along the stream's bank, the ground dappled by the fading sunlight as it filtered through the boughs of willows. He sat for a while, thinking, until his mind became a blank screen and for a while he too, like the earth, was peaceful.

It would be so good, he thought, to let it all go. Perhaps the wounds would someday heal by themselves if they were not reopened. How good it would be if life could always be as it was now, by the stream's bank. He would go back to Elizabeth and hold her and love her, genuinely, openly, and make what they had shared that morning last for the rest of their lives. It was possible. More than anything, it was this that he wanted. But more than what he wanted, was the sense of what he owed his father. Loyalty bound him and took precedence over all else.

The peace gave way to a melancholia as deep as the indigo shadows settling around him. Weighted by the mood, he pulled himself up from the ground and continued to walk farther along the bank.

His walk ended at a site of ruin. It wasn't his first visit since he had moved back. Previously, he had spent several days there, measuring and sketching out plans, going over projected costs on everything from new machinery to the cost of insurance, to the wages he would have to offer workers. But no matter how many times he came, the response of outrage was still the same. It was why he found it so necessary now to be there, on this evening when his resolve was weak, and the desire to throw in the towel and greedily take something for himself and forget the others, was strong.

So he stood there, like a warrior with his legs spread, surveying what miseries the past had wrought.

Thirteen years had passed, yet distress still hovered over the charred siding and partially capsized roof of the main structure. By a trick of inner vision Cade saw it as it had been thirteen years ago: the shining hope of his father. The Delaney mill, it had been called. How proud he had been whenever the title had been spoken, for to him it had signified the triumph of good over evil. He'd been still naive and idealistic enough to believe that things always came out right side up. Well, he had been wrong about that, hadn't he?

He entered the crumbling structure and examined it for the toll that time and the deliberate acts of men had taken. There was really very little left to remind him of the past he had known; inside, the building reflected the same empty shell that the outside had promised it to be. If he tried, he could place in his mind where the machinery had been. He could hear his father's voice, see the other men and women moving through the now deserted spaces—spaces which would once again be filled before he left town.

In New York he had been less impassioned. Removed in distance from Greenridge he could better maintain his objectivity, which supported the decision to purchase a new site for the mill he would build. The location of his father's factory had been ill chosen, its selection predicated primarily on what he could afford at the time and by what land was made available to him. Proctor Huntington had done all he could to block his father's bid to compete. Using his social and economic clout, Huntington had seen to it that property that had previously been for sale became mysteriously unavailable.

But since Cade had returned, he had let sentimentality and hatred rule over his better judgment. He would build his mill here. He would use the very foundation on which the first mill had been constructed, and shore up the walls with every scrap of lumber he could salvage from the original structure. Like the mythical Phoenix, his father's dream would rise in form from ashes. He would see to it.

For the rest of the night he remained on the site. With his back against a wall, he sat staring into the dark stillness. Mostly he was awake, although he might have dozed periodically. In the distance he heard the wail and thunder of passing trains. And over and over, his thoughts were drawn back to that morning when he had been with Elizabeth. His body would tremble, grow hot with a need he had never before experienced for any woman, and he would force himself to recall who she was—the daughter of his father's destroyer—and to remember that he had made the journey back to this town to possess her and destroy her, as her father had done to his own. Twice a squirrel, or perhaps it was something more sinister, scampered close by his feet; and at the earliest light, the bats returned from their nocturnal scavenging to hang on the decaying rafters.

Finally, he drew himself up, and prepared to return to his room. The weariness and the night of remembrances had rendered him invulnerable to Elizabeth's feminine spell.

Chapter Seven

Elizabeth stood with her face pressed against the door, listening for the man, the veritable stranger with whom she had made love the previous morning. As she did, she suddenly saw herself as in a film, with another part of herself also serving as the audience. The woman she observed was a clear fool, a silly thing who did not recognize the tryst for what it had been: no more than an animal thing between a virile male and a lonely woman with her own sexual longings. The woman—pathetic creature!—was trying to turn the experience into a grand romantic encounter.

She hated what she saw! Hated it because it was so clearly the truth. The truth always hurt. And the truth pained her ego mightily.

The camera of Elizabeth's mind moved relentlessly to the other side of the door where the man—the object of her misguided obsession—was coolly removed from all such concerns and illusions.

This she saw, too. She could not look away from it. It was fascinatingly, horribly instructive, this overview of the relationship as seen from an objective perspective.

In her mind's eye, he strode past the door, assured, self-involved, and thinking of other matters. Unlike her, he was unencumbered by sexual and emotional longing. He had probably—no, certainly—spent the night with another woman. Otherwise, where else could he have been?

It was this thought, like a slap startling her out of hysteria, that drew Elizabeth back into herself and propelled her, in self-disgust, to withdraw from the door.

In a moment she heard the door to his room open and close, and in another moment the sound of the shower running.

He had not hesitated at her door. He had not even thought of her! He was cold clear through, and she would do well to remember that.

Opposite where she stood, she caught her reflection in the oval mirror of the dressing table. The blue eyes looking back were not those of a seething temptress of men, but of a woman who was weary and confused and frightened. Strands of pale hair, damp from the humidity, clung to her temples and lay in flat wisps of defeat against the sides of her face.

What had she been thinking of all night? She must have been temporarily mad to have thought there was anything between them. The heat was the cause. It was the damned, infernal heat with its even more unbearable humidity making it impossible to breathe, impossible to think straight, impossible to live.

With a sense of aimlessness, she crossed the room, a vague notion in her mind to view the sky for a hopeful sign that relief was on the way. On the balcony the sun already scorched and she drew back slightly into the shade cast by the open shuttered doors. There they were: the same white clouds already growing into their formidable shapes, just as they had every morning since summer began. The backdrop of sky was a radiant blue. Below, the earth had lost its green and was fast becoming a brittle landscape of brown and beige vegetation. It was, she thought, gazing out over her property, as if the same slow-spreading blight that had affected her life was now seeping into the landscape, staining what had been paradise. Even the leaves on the row of venerable oaks leading up the drive to her house were beginning to singe.

No wonder she was behaving oddly; all of nature was out of sorts. Why should she be any exception?

Anyway, she decided, turning away from the blistering heat and shutting the doors after her, she had to be realistic. There was no other choice but to give up her mournful romanticizing and go on with her life as it had been before Cade Delaney had taken a jog off the main road and wheeled into her placid existence, turning it upside down and inside out. And reducing her to her present state.

Just thinking of it brought forth a genuine sigh of emotional exhaustion. But, weary or not, she would start again with her life, picking up where she had left off before the insane interlude with her boarder.

She allowed herself one last sigh, and then, determined and desperate to maintain her sense of purpose, she gathered together the tools she would use to regain control of her wits, and thereby her life. From a messy pile of papers accumulated over the past couple of days, she retrieved a couple of pens, a lined yellow pad, and the latest financial statement prepared by her chief accountant.

With her booty, she sat down on her bed and spread everything before her like a feast. Just the sight of such intended future productivity raised her spirits.

Amid all the uncertainty, there was one absolute she could count on: life would continue—with or without her. She may as well try to keep pace.

Holding to that thought, she waved a mental goodbye to the man in the other room, the man she would no longer acknowledge as being important to her life, the man who had just turned off the shower. Before she knew it was happening, a brief image of his wet hard body slipped through her screen of resolve.

She was quick on the rebound. Grasping the ballpoint pen, she wrote in large determined letters across the top of the pad: Things to Do Today.

And then, desperate to save herself from further imaginings, she proceeded to do them.

At ten that morning, she was in a better frame of mind. She was determined to turn the mill operation around. Only occasionally during the morning had her mind strayed from its purpose, as she examined again and again the latest financial report on the company, each time searching for creative ways to cut corners and turn a profit. It was imperative that the mill make some money fast.

It was almost noon when she decided—partially as a protective measure—to drive to the factory. That would keep her out of the house and away from Cade Delaney should he begin to stir about. Besides, she had ideas to share with the plant manager and controller. She knew they both resented her interference, since they usually took only the barest of pains to conceal their feelings. Any input she had ever offered to improve the plant's operation had been greeted with condescension. Well, that was too bad for them, Elizabeth concluded, steeling herself for her next charge into the fray. They really had no choice but to swallow her advice, be it brilliant, as she thought, or simplistic and inane, as they held. She was still the sole owner.

She was almost out the door when, to her surprise, Mason Philips's white Cadillac turned off the road. While she watched, it took a long, slow approach up the driveway and finally cruised to a stop.

"Mason!" she greeted. The screen door slammed after her as she went out onto the veranda.

Stepping out of the Cadillac, he was a creature of studied Southern elegance. His suit was white and his shirt a pale blue. The tie he wore swirled with pale pastels, pinks, greens, blue, a soft yellow. The shoes were soft white loafers, eelskin. To Elizabeth, he looked too clean, too antiseptic, bland. Once she had found him reasonably appealing. Now things were different. Her tastes were more educated since Cade's arrival.

Mason, a man without fire, she thought, considering his total effect on her now. A man of mush. A contrasting image of Cade grew before her, hungry green eyes blazing in the light of the moon, that tight, curious edge to him that colored each moment spent in his presence with a sense of compelling, addictive danger. A familiar rush coursed through her, and in one beat of her heart she burned from desire, and in the next drowned in a dark well of hopelessness. It was never, never to be. She must remember that. She must.

Mason turned, looking to the house as she called him.

"Elizabeth..." he returned, and seemed about to say something more, but his attention became immediately distracted. Elizabeth followed the direction of his interest to the green car parked to the side and near her own—Cade's car.

"This *is* a surprise," she called, waiting in the shade of the veranda.

Still rooted by the Cadillac, he trained his attention back on her again. "Probably should have called. Forgive me. I was out and about, and just took the chance I'd find you home," Mason offered. "Haven't seen you in a while, Elizabeth. I worry that you're doing all right."

His face smiled, but the eyes did not bear a corresponding warmth. She recognized the statement for what it was—a rebuke, thinly veiled, because everything with Mason was a disguise of some sort. All the elite of Greenridge were covered in a haze of social refinement. She herself had once wafted about with her own gossamer armor to protect her from too much reality.

"But I must say, you're looking lovely, as usual," Mason was going on. That, at least, she knew was true. In spite of everything she felt, she'd somehow managed to pull her outside self together; it was part of her valiant attempt to be reborn from emotional purgatory.

"I was just about to leave," she said, hoping the announcement might cut short their visit. Besides, she knew Mason too well to believe he ever did anything by impulse. There had to be a reason for the visit and she wasn't in the frame of mind to war over money owed to the bank or dodge his romantic advances. She just wanted to get out, to move forward in her life.

After Cade had come home at last, and she had reconciled herself to the fact of the one-night stand, she had put away the few dishes left over from her boarders' breakfasts and then retired to her room again, where she had bathed for the second time that day. After long and serious deliberation, she'd dressed in a cool yellow suit, the sleeves short, the wide yellow belt with its silver buckle giving her a wasp waist and lending a gentle, flowing line to her hips. She knew she might appear too provocatively feminine for the factory, but she had no money to invest in more appropriate wear; so it was either outfits like this, or slacks, which she felt undermined what little professional dignity she possessed. To compensate for the cheerful inappropriateness of the dress, she had modestly drawn her hair back and fastened it into an ivory clip at the nape of her neck.

She went on with her explanation. "You know how much I love visiting with you, Mason. But the trouble is—"

"Well, I know I should have called," Mason broke in before she could develop a good case on her own behalf. "But like I said, I just took the chance I'd catch you in. Guess I was lucky. Doesn't seem right to let good fortune slide right out from under you, does it? Even though sometimes it does just that. Here you are, on your way out, and I come around just in the nick of time." His voice was liquid silk in the heat. Mason himself was liquid silk, a shimmering apparition without substance.

There was something odd in his manner. It was not in what he said, Elizabeth considered, but in what he was not saying. Even in their brief interchange, his eyes had drifted from her face off to the side again, to the car, and later wandered past her to the screen door, as if he were searching for something hidden.

"Mason, is there something wrong?" She wondered if she had managed to keep the mockery from her voice, then decided she was too hot to care, anyway. Let him be offended. Let the whole world gasp at her rudeness.

"No." He seemed caught by surprise. "No, not at all," he went on, quickly recovered.

"I just thought there might be something troubling you."

"Why, what made you think that?" His face had re-settled into a bland pudding. Any truth at all would stick in that goo, never to be released.

"Well, I guess, Mason, what it is . . . you seem a little distracted."

"Ummm, yes, I might at that," he said, somewhat more animated, like a schoolboy who had correctly an-swered a question he hadn't anticipated. "The heat." He made an issue of swiping at his brow with a hand-kerchief taken from his pants pocket. Squinting to-ward Elizabeth, he said, "Hellish, isn't it, this heat? Summer's never going to end. And if I used the good sense the Lord gave me, I'd get right out of that devil sun." He laughed at himself, and strode to the veranda where Elizabeth waited in what shade existed beneath the overhang of the front balcony.

"I keep hoping for rain," she said. "But of course the blue just lasts and lasts."

Mason nodded gravely. "Can't ever recall a summer like this one. Everyone's saying that. This whole summer's one that never should have happened."

"No," she said quietly, thinking first of Edward, and then reflecting on more than her widowhood, "it hasn't been the best of all summers."

Mason misinterpreted her thoughts.

"I didn't mean to bring up... I'm sorry, Elizabeth. I'm deeply sorry. Stupid of me. It wasn't to remind you."

She went along with his error. Would it have been better to tell him the truth? That she was very depressed because she had wanted to make love with a stranger until she couldn't see straight anymore? That this stranger didn't want her for some reason, and so now all she had in her life was a broken-down mill and a milksop dandy in a white suit who had come to call on her? No, it would not have been a good thing to tell the truth.

"Please, Mason. I can't go on grieving forever now, can I?"

"No, of course not. And Elizabeth, I feel I must tell you. You're the finest, most brave woman I've ever known for having adopted that kind of realistic attitude."

Again she noted that even in the brief space of this last exchange of pleasantries, his eyes had been drawn beyond her, seeking something out of view. Resignedly, she offered the invitation she knew she must. "Why not come in for a while? There's some iced tea already made."

"Well, thank you, Elizabeth. That would be very nice. As long as I don't hold you up."

"Of course not. You know you're always my most welcome guest, Mason. Our long friendship is a cornerstone of my life." If she could say that with a straight face, she was capable of anything. Anyway, she had suddenly, unexpectedly become more interested in conversing with Mason. The mystery was building as to what had really brought him to her doorstep. Mysteries seemed to hold a special place in her life lately.

He waited for her in the large formal drawing room while she fetched a tray with glasses of iced tea, and brought it to him garnished with sprigs of mint from what was left of the garden. Like her, mint seemed to survive everything whether or not it really cared to.

"I hope it's cold enough," she said, the sweet domestic voice she had cultivated over the years rising to the surface. The inflection of her voice made her sick. She smiled as Mason accepted the drink.

He took a sip. She saw how his gaze had again drifted beyond the room. He was looking through the opened window out to the drive. "New boarder?" he asked after another thoughtful swallow. "The car out there," he explained. "It belongs to a new boarder?"

She wondered at the question. Was this merely small talk before the real topic presented itself? Or, was there some point to be made? "He's been here a while," Elizabeth answered.

"Ummm, that so?" An unfathomable note of hostility had crept into Mason's usual Milquetoast delivery.

"Yes."

Mason took a long swallow. He looked up suddenly. "Who is he, Elizabeth?"

The question, as well as the look he hurled across the room, was sharp. He might have been a grand inquisitor and she a woman with a crime to hide.

"Just a man," she replied warily. "From New York."

"And?" Mason waited. "Surely there's more to him."

She took out her sprig of mint, played with it, twirled it around, then punched it back between two ice cubes. She did not want to talk about Cade. Shrugging, she said, "That's it. Just a man from New York. He has some business to finish up in Greenridge and then he'll be gone."

"Oh? And when's that going to be?"

"I really don't see that this is worth talking about, Mason."

God help her. Already, just in the brief discussion they were having about Cade Delaney, she could feel the sense of excitement arise, and if by the mention of his name she was summoning him into her life again. Her cheeks burned. To hide her discomfort, she turned away from Mason and busied herself with a candy dish, which she repositioned on a different table.

"It's just that in your present situation, you don't seem to be thinking too clearly, Elizabeth. I worry."

Mason's voice had dipped lower and was laced with the tones of a critical father. The statements reminded her of Edward, who would periodically express his pique in such a fashion. The implication was that she was either in danger of embarrassing herself or them by not living up to some vaguely defined "good girl" standard.

"Perhaps it's the heat," she said. She made no particular effort to hide the sarcasm. "It's melted the marbles in my head."

"Or perhaps you've just never acquainted yourself with the ways of this world enough to know better," Mason said sharply.

"Better than what?" Elizabeth shot back, truly feeling outrage.

"A woman in your position does not just open her doors wide to a man she doesn't know."

"My doors?" She raised one brow. "Come now...we're both adults. Why not be more direct, Mason."

"Elizabeth—" he cautioned.

"It's not my doors you're speaking of, is it, Mason?"

Clearly he had not expected that kind of boldness from her. He blanched.

"I've met the man, Elizabeth," Mason explained with the underlying impatience of someone who was attempting to be cool when he would rather have thrashed about and created a cyclone of a scene. "I know the kind well."

"Really? And what kind is that?" It was her turn to be suddenly alarmed at the direction the talk had taken. She did not really want to know about Cade's life, not any more than she already knew. There was enough pain in that.

She would be content to let the relationship end with her fantasies and illusions intact. Let it all be what she imagined—no more and no less, and let there be a loud "Amen" at the end of the entire affair when he drove out of her life the same way he had come into it.

"He's the kind who takes women as toys," Mason said viciously. "He plays with them and later on discards them like so much trash."

Her face had grown very hot, as if ants were stinging her, and she must have turned a corresponding crimson, for suddenly Mason was looking at her queerly with a sort of triumphant condemning rage that also held fear. "Elizabeth?"

The accusation was implicit in the single utterance of her name.

A sickening feeling had come to the pit of her stomach. A shaking had joined it, and she had the urge to cry in self-pity. She suppressed a fierce impulse to run screaming up the stairs and beat at Cade's door and rake his face raw with her nails. She had been used. And she hated him! She had wanted him, desired him with her whole being—such a fool, she was! And all the time, she had been no more than another stupid, insignificant roll in the hay. A plush receptacle for his male libido! Oh, she had known it, known it, earlier that morning. Of course. But now...to have the truth flung in her face like some odious heap of manure by Mason...it was too much to bear.

She stood suddenly. Her legs felt like rubber bands. She breathed deeply, trying to keep enough presence about her to hide her humiliation. "That's a truly disgusting thing to say, Mason." And it was—precisely because it was true.

Overall Mason looked pleased, as if he had just claimed some sort of advantage. He looked as though he was about to say something, but the words died unspoken as his attention moved to the door. At what he saw, his expression faded to uncertainty, and Elizabeth turned to see why.

"Good morning," Cade said mildly, slanting a look from her to Mason. He leaned against the doorframe in an unsettled stance, as though ready to take off in the next breath.

Elizabeth imagined mockery in the greeting, but couldn't be sure. There did seem to be obvious amusement playing behind the green eyes. That, at least was something. Rarely had she seen him display even this much emotion in a social situation. He'd always been guarded. But what did he guard? Always a question behind another question.

In this case, however, she decided he could not resist the impulse to react as the humor was at her expense. Obviously, he must have heard enough of the conversation to be entertained. His reaction was self-congratulatory, like a thief who had finally been caught after pulling off a daring burglary. There was no shame over the crime, but pleasure over having his cleverness finally revealed.

"Good morning," she said stiffly, reluctant to look at Cade for long, for fear of what her own eyes would show. "I understand you two have already become acquainted."

"Yes, we've had that pleasure," Cade said as he strolled farther into the room.

This morning, Elizabeth noted, he had not dressed in his more usual uniform of jeans and work shirt. His slacks were beige, and expensive by the cut and material. He wore a light blue dress shirt, a tie, and carried an unstructured off-white raw silk jacket, which dangled from his hand by the collar. If he had been out all night catting it up, the cat must have done him a lot of good. Clean shaven and bright of eye, he matched perfectly the expression "radiant." A white-hot bolt of lightning jealousy drove through Elizabeth as she thought of the means by which he had come by that glow. If the summer had not been good, this morning was a disaster.

"Really?" Elizabeth said. "And where was that?"

"It was at the Greenridge Inn," Mason said, rushing in with the information, as if he were a player attempting to take control of the field before the other side could gain a foothold. "Mr. Delaney and his . . ." Here Mason broke off, as if searching for another, more polite word to use rather than the one coming immediately to mind. "Mr. Delaney and his companion," Mason continued, "were at the bar together." Clearly this information was meant to further discourage Elizabeth from entertaining any romantic notions about her handsome boarder.

Cade only laughed; just two regular guys sharing a male joke together. "Greenridge women do seem to have a certain welcoming way for strangers."

Mason's face turned the shade of gray mold. "Not all women, surely." The statement was a clear warning for Cade to back away from his implication.

"Certainly not." Cade grinned back conspiratorily to Mason. Elizabeth burned, but pretended she did not quite catch the allusion. If he had also winked, Elizabeth would not have been surprised. Everything he was doing was purposeful; she knew him well enough to know that, at least.

She stepped slightly away, a subtle physical declaration of her independence from the production under way. Cade would also understand that. She doubted seriously if anything that occurred in his presence was lost to him. To Elizabeth, that gift of observation served to make him both more attractive and more deadly.

"But I wouldn't be interested in just any woman," Cade countered. "It's only the most beautiful who are worth all the trouble they eventually cause a man." He looked pointedly at Elizabeth.

She met his mirth with her hardest look. His smile widened engagingly and she looked away, discounting it and him.

The two men were using her as a piece of meat to be torn apart in their verbal joust of male egos. But even here, in her own living room, she was in dangerous territory. There was no way to know how far Cade would go in his bid to win in his match against Mason. Would he tell Mason they had spent a rousing time in bed only the day before? Would he go that far? Then, again, a part of her would not have minded that at all. She'd be free of Mason forever. For all time, by all of Greenridge, she would be branded a fallen woman. They would strike her from the social register—which she did not care about anyway. But on the down side, men like Jake Fenster would parade boldly to her doorstep, rather than creep about her as they did now. That she would not want.

So she held her tongue, and wished to God that Mason would as well, but he didn't. Instead, he suddenly came alive and waved the dusty standard of Southern chivalry.

"I don't appreciate your insinuations, sir."

"I don't recall having made an insinuation about you, sir," Cade returned with contrasting good humor.

"I am not speaking of myself."

"No, of course not." Cade looked at Elizabeth. Where before a sort of demonic glee had characterized his expression, a shift had occurred in the green focus of his eyes. Elizabeth detected the softening, and was confused by it. But then he always confused her.

"Then I suggest you retract what you have suggested."

"Mason," Elizabeth intervened quickly, "I think that this has truly gone far enough."

Mason's face grew darker. "I agree. Much too far, I should think. It will be dropped. Now."

"I'm terribly sorry, Mrs. Hart, if I've in any way offended you. I was merely speaking generally, of course. I've found Southern hospitality extremely warm. Women here have a certain instinct for femininity which their sisters in other parts of the country seem to have misplaced."

"We do try to make guests feel welcome. Speaking generally, of course. Our friendliness is inbred. Nothing personal."

Mason looked from Elizabeth to Cade, then back again to Elizabeth and, finding an opening, threw a wedge into the conversation, which seemed on several levels at once, none of which had anything to do with him. "Will you have dinner with me tonight, Elizabeth?"

She hesitated. Both men's eyes were on her, as if whatever she were to say would decide something that went far beyond a dinner invitation. She was to choose sides, and thus declare the victor.

For a moment she remained absolutely frozen in indecision. If she were to go to dinner with Mason, she realized she was virtually condemning herself to a progressive relationship with him. Now, this moment, was the time to cut everything off between them cleanly. His pride would be battered and he would hate her, but she would be free of his overtures forever after. On the other hand, Mason held the loan papers to the mill and if she lost his goodwill she might easily lose her factory. There was no guarantee she would be able to pull off saving the mill, but at least with Mason on her side, it improved her chances. A dinner with him could buy some more time. Naturally, he knew that. Mason was no fool. But neither was she, and that is why he had asked. It was his trump card.

And what of Cade? There was nothing there for her but sexual fulfillment; the rest of the relationship consisted of a lot of yearning on her part and a great deal of distance on his. She wanted far more emotionally than this man could deliver. One day he would drive away, and then she would be left with memories. She could see herself standing on the veranda, waiting night after night after night for headlights that would never reappear.

"Yes," she answered suddenly. "Dinner tonight would be lovely."

"Good," Mason said, "then I'll be by at seven." He looked briefly to Cade, who smiled back.

It was a chilling smile, and definitely not one belonging to a loser. Mason's own expression changed slightly. He seemed less sure of his victory.

There was a space of silence between the three of them, and then awkwardly, like a man who had sensed his presence was intrusive, Mason made the noises of departure. "Well, I have to be on my way, meeting with Jim Speggers and George Lightfoot about the new tractor store they're setting up." He broke off. "I'll be by for you at seven."

"I'll be looking forward to tonight," she said, for the benefit of Cade.

Mason's departure seemed to take forever. For the effect of good public relations, she stood at the window and waved a final goodbye to him.

When she turned, Cade had slipped away, his mission accomplished. He had merely stopped by long enough to sully whatever relationship she might have going with Mason.

And in the interim, her enthusiasm for visiting the mill had waned. She had to force herself to follow through with her original plans. Outside, as she opened the car door, she glanced briefly up at the house and found Cade watching her from just inside his room.

Chapter Eight

That evening, Elizabeth dressed carefully for her dinner engagement with Mason. The dress she selected was a soft pink sheath. The color would make her appear vulnerable and the style alluring yet appropriately reserved. That was important, that she appear every inch the lady. The neckline would hint at her feminine charms, but would not scream with blatant sexuality. Earrings were simple pearl drops and the bracelet of pearls and diamonds, a former anniversary gift, was properly delicate and rich.

She despised all the premeditated cunning, even as she took each measure—and yes, they were measures, precautions. Her afternoon visit to the mill had been the rotten cherry at the top of a perfectly rotten day. Not only had she quarreled with the plant manager, but the controller had given his resignation. He found the circumstances demoralizing, and for his own peace of mind wanted out. He suggested she think seriously about doing the same. There was a rumor that the bank was going to foreclose, anyway.

In her gay yellow dress, previously worn to so many pleasant social occasions where laughter had been the order of the day, she had stood in the dingy office, feeling silly with the sheet she made up earlier that listed her possible solutions to turn the mill around.

Neither of the men had been particularly cruel, nor even condescending this time. It was as if they had finally come to accept her as a strange aberration in their lives, and had ceased to be surprised or offended or even intrigued by her. She was merely a weird fact to be dealt with as infrequently as possible, with only the least personal involvement necessary.

"We don't have the money to go against the competition," the manager had said. "We don't have the sales team. We can't even afford to pay for supplies in quantities that will give us the price break to produce fabric that will be competitive on the market. We've had to let go of two-thirds of our labor force. This may sound like a cruel thing to say, Mrs. Hart, but I think it would be to your advantage to face facts. Your husband is dead. And so is this operation."

And she had to agree with him—in principle.

But, as long as the machines still worked, and as long as she still had them, she would try to hold on to her family's heritage and what might be her only chance at a decent livelihood.

Mason was therefore her last and only hope.

Maybe that was why she had grown to despise him so, because of her dependency. However, it could be more than that, she'd thought, as she'd bathed before the dinner engagement. It could very well be that she had

changed so much over the past few months that she saw
him and all the others as they really were: odious, su-
perficial opportunists who exploited their social and
economic inferiors. Through lack of perspective, she
supposed she had once been exactly like them. She remembered Aggie on her last day, and could now understand much better the woman's resentment. Aggie
had seen her as careless, and she had been—just as Edward had been in his own way.

But whether or not she disapproved of Mason, she
still needed him to buy time.

So she bathed and perfumed and powdered herself,
and fluffed her long hair so that it curled under lightly
at her shoulders, and when Mason's car turned into the
drive at precisely seven o'clock, she was ready to pretend she was the woman she had once been.

Cade stood at his door leading to the balcony. He was
just out of view, yet he could see clearly. And he could
hear. The laughter was like small silver bells to his ears
as he watched Elizabeth climb into the Cadillac. He remembered that lilting jingle so well from when he had
been a boy. Even then he had loved it and abhorred it.
How he had worshiped her! She of the soft golden hair
and the arresting blue eyes, the skin as smooth and un-
flawed as rich cream, the voice that purred promises of
paradise rather than mere words. But the words were
spoken always to others. Just as they were now.

How he had longed to know what she had said to
those privileged others. He used to invent in his mind
whole dialogues of what had transpired in these sacred
social discourses. What information had been exchanged that made those of her set throw back their

heads in glee, or nod sagely, the fortunate recipients of
her mysterious feminine wisdom and tantalizing wit?

There was so much of her that he wanted to possess!
And in wanting that, he hated her even more. There was
the burning, the constant searing pain in his heart, an
amalgam of love and fury. Like two ferocious animals
trapped and fighting for their lives within him, they
gnawed and clawed in the dark pit that was his miserable soul.

And there she was again, as she had always been, the
magnificent, perfect, Elizabeth, laughing, her head
thrown back in the same way she had tilted it when she
was a teenager. Then, as now, he had watched her un-
detected from a distance. He had not been out of sight
then, but in full view had any one cared to look. They
had not. Chandon Delaney had gone unnoticed for the
sheer reason that he was of no importance to the group
over which Elizabeth presided. He had belonged to the
faceless, nameless group whose fathers and mothers
worked as day laborers in the mill, or in the fields, or as
domestics in the large houses.

From just inside his room, he watched Mason climb
into his car next to her. He saw Mason reach across and
touch the side of her face with affection. The car's
windows were open and he heard that light laughter
again, and each note of it cut into his gut.

Turning from the scene, he moved into the darkness
that had begun to fill his room. There was a fifth of
bourbon on his dresser and he quickly poured himself
a glass and downed it as the sound of the Cadillac's engine faded down the road.

For a long while he sat on the edge of his bed, thinking and finishing another full glass of bourbon. His
mind did not turn fuzzy as he had hoped. Instead, it

seemed sharp and hurtful as a razor's edge tearing away at him.

He had not triumphed over Elizabeth, quite simply because she did not know it was he. To Elizabeth the man who had taken her body was a man from New York who had blown into town with fine clothes and a late-model car and some mysterious purpose to accomplish. The anonymity was necessary to carry out his whole plan.

But until she knew it was him—the Chandon Delaney who had been invisible all of those years when she had been the brightest light in his life—he would never end the torment. He would never truly win. She would always be out of reach, no matter how many times he made love to her.

But he was determined. There would come a time when he would make love to her and she would look into his eyes with the knowledge of his true identity. And then, and only then, could he laugh and be free. She would know that he had crossed into her realm and that he had plundered her world the way her father had his.

The mill was an integral part of the total plan. He needed both Elizabeth and the mill to make his revenge complete.

The liquor and the thought of the future revitalized him, and the next few hours passed quickly as he worked on the final plans for the mill. Everything was in order, ready to be implemented. He would begin work in less than a week.

It could have been a matter of only minutes since Elizabeth had left the house with Mason, so absorbed had he been in his work. The sound of the car coming up the road and then turning slowly down the drive came into Cade's consciousness as though through a time warp, pulling him from one world back into the other. He glanced at his watch. It was after one o'clock in the morning.

One o'clock? The implications of the time Elizabeth had spent away with Mason stunned him. Up to this point, he had not been overly concerned with the dinner engagement. That was a relatively safe affair. Mason wasn't hot-blooded enough to cause him concern. He knew another man's sexual style, just as he sensed how far a particular woman might go. That knowledge made things easier at times, but it also spoiled things. Women had ceased to be a challenge to him—except for Elizabeth. She was a known quantity in certain ways, and unknown in others. The fact was, he sometimes wondered who she was. Like him, she seemed not quite who she had once been, but not quite who she yet was becoming.

But Mason Philips he did know. He was a cold bastard, with ice in his veins. He would not make a false move with Elizabeth. If he went after her—which he was clearly doing—it would be in a slow and certain way, with each step plotted.

He knew Mason was not the kind of man to lose control over a woman's body and risk blowing his whole scene. What Philips really lusted over was prestige and power. And Elizabeth could give that to him.

Cade left his desk and moved to the window. The Cadillac was parked in the drive and the lights were out. Only the dimmest shadows moved within the car, but the figures appeared to be close together.

Cade waited. Outside there was the roll of distant thunder, almost too faint to be noticed. Then all was quiet again. There was the rasp of frogs not yet dead from the drought, the continuous buzz like an on-going electrical current from the crickets, and the off-again, on-again burst of light from fireflies. Still he waited. The heat closed in on him, the air heavy with moisture. He drew his damp shirt off and flung it to the bed, all the while watching the car for movement.

It suddenly occurred to him that he had been too smug. What if he had underestimated Mason Philips? What if Philips had skipped several moves and had gone past "Go" on his quest to own the best real estate in Greenridge.

As he thought it, the door of the Cadillac opened and the object of Cade's inquiry stepped onto the drive. Mason moved around the car to let Elizabeth out. They stood together for a moment and talked in low voices. Then Elizabeth began to back away. Mason came forward a few steps, but she said something to him that Cade could not make out, and Mason remained where he was.

Cade watched Mason as Mason watched Elizabeth, who headed to the house. The curving feminine promise of her body was clear and provocative in the sheath dress. Cade experienced an instant stirring of desire to feel her beneath him again.

Downstairs the door closed softly. Mason turned back to the Cadillac, hesitated, and then started back for the house, moving rapidly.

Jesus, Cade thought, *he's really going to go for it.*

There was no question of what needed to be done. He was across the room and into the hall even before the front door had again swung closed.

Elizabeth was standing just inside the door when Cade descended the staircase. Mason was near her, his hand pressed against the small of her back, and the other entwined in her hair. In his mind, Cade played out the rapid sequence of seduction to follow the initial moves. They were in every male's repertoire, simple and effective and learned at the onset of puberty from rampaging hormones and abetted by locker-room talk. Only this time the infallible game plan was not going to work, because he was not going to allow it.

He took no particular care to make his entrance one of stealth, nor did he make enough noise so everyone could avoid embarrassment. He simply arrived in the most normal way.

And what he had meant to do, he accomplished. The heated little tableau dissolved at his entrance. Elizabeth's eyes blazed brilliantly as she turned to the sound of his footsteps. Whether this inner fire was brought about by lust or fury or humiliation, Cade could not tell. He also realized suddenly that it was important that he know. The idea, crazy as it was, that she might have actually have wanted Mason...would have actually considered... It was a disagreeable notion.

Cade broke his journey just short of the ground floor, hovering four steps above them. For a moment the three of them merely stared at each other.

Having won the round, Cade felt generous. "Oh, sorry. Bad timing. I heard sounds and..."

"Do you always creep down the stairs when someone comes in at night?" Mason commented testily.

"No," Elizabeth said dryly. "He's usually not here. Are you, Mr. Delaney?"

Cade nodded and smiled. "No, I also dine out until very late. They have some excellent desserts in the early hours. I'm sure you agree with that, Mason."

"Just what are you implying?"

"It can mean whatever you think," Cade returned, but there was a decided lack of easy humor in the last volley. "Maybe it just means you were having one hell of a dinner. Or maybe it means that you're one terrific conversationalist. It's none of my business either way. I woke up when I heard the door open and close—twice. In New York you don't lie around waiting for your neck to be sliced. You check out the scene and decide your options. Are you going to run or fight? And sometimes you find you may not have any options."

There had been a secondary message in what he had said. By the change in Mason's face, Cade figured he had gotten it. When the other man spoke, Cade was certain. He was glad Mason wasn't dumb. It made everything much easier.

"I guess the important thing is to decide if you're being outmatched."

Cade laughed. "Did you say outmatched or outclassed?"

"In some situations, they turn out to be one and the same."

"Well, class doesn't count for a whole hell of a lot on the mean streets."

"That's maybe why I live here in the country."

"Good for you, Philips. But have you ever heard of urban sprawl? It's everywhere. Just creeps in on nice places like this and mucks everything up. Damn shame, isn't it?" Cade shook his head disparagingly.

"We've got a lot of modern ways of dealing with all kinds of contamination," Mason returned. "And some of the old ways work just as well."

"Yeah, well, practice makes perfect. I'm sure you refer to the good ol' boy style of handling problems. People in the city read about those little stunts in books, and think they're just fairy tales. Some people who don't know better believe those kinds of things only happen in the movies—a group of mad dog men come down on some poor sonofabitch who doesn't want to go along with the established order of things. Isn't that what we're talking about?''

"Who are you?" Mason asked quietly. He took a step forward, as if to get a closer look and unmask the mystery.

"Just another one of Elizabeth's boarders. Just a man from New York passing through. No one to worry about."

Mason shook his head, but he didn't pursue the inquiry further. Cade was certain he would. And that was okay. It was getting around the time when he would be laying down his cards, anyway. And in the meantime, it made him feel good to know that he was causing Mason some preliminary discomfort.

In Mason, Cade recognized the faces of all the men who had gone after his father. It was a different face, but the same man. They were interchangeable entities, men like Proctor Huntington and this suitor of Elizabeth's.

"You watch yourself now, you hear?" Mason said, and began to back toward the door again.

To Elizabeth, he said, "I'm sorry for all this. It's ugly. A woman shouldn't have to hear ugly things. I'll do what I can to see that things in your life get cleaned up and put back into the right kind of order." He sent Cade a bald look of hatred. "Elizabeth, you think more about what we talked about." He brushed her face with one finger. "Will you be all right here?"

"Yes, of course," she said. "This is my house. I'll be all right."

Mason cast one more parting look at Cade, a dark glance filled with all the twisting danger of a snake pit. "I'll call you tomorrow," Mason said to Elizabeth, then left with a theatrical flourish that left the screen door rattling afterward.

Elizabeth had not spoken, nor moved, during the heated interchange. Now as she turned, Cade read cold fury in her eyes.

"I want you out of here tomorrow," she said. "You have no right—"

But Cade had begun to move down the steps to her, and grabbed her before the sentence was out. His mouth came against hers, silencing the rest of the speech.

Elizabeth's mouth opened to his automatically, as if she had no will of her own, and his tongue flicked hot against hers, exploring and pushing in the same insinuating rhythm as his hips spiraled against her.

"No...no..." she moaned, struggling, but he pushed her back against the nearest wall and kissed the hollow of her neck.

"It's over with us," she breathed. "Stop...it's finished, Cade."

When she tried again to escape, he took both her hands in one of his. He pinned them up above her head as he pressed himself more insistently against her. Her breath was ragged, and only part of her resisted as his mouth slid over the top of her breasts, hardening her nipples.

It was all he could do not to throw her down on the ground and raise her skirt over her hips. He had never wanted a woman as much as he desired this one. The feelings he had were all spinning one on top of the other, lust and hate and the urge to dominate and a release of the river of love that had coursed through him those many years.

"Did he make love to you, Elizabeth?" he asked, the question a taunt. He felt suddenly cruel. It was absurd. For so many years he had been a hostage to this single soft creature. She had ruled over his life for far too long. He wanted her exposed as less than she was in his fantasies so that he might exorcise her once and for all.

She was quiet, almost completely still, and so was he as they both waited.

"Tell me," Cade ordered. He backed away slightly and cupped her chin, tilting her face to see into her eyes. "Did you let him make love to you?"

"Yes," she said simply.

Cade smiled. "No . . . no, he didn't. He didn't even touch you." Arrogantly, he traced a finger lightly over the high swell of bosom.

She jerked away, and he allowed her the momentary escape from his attentions. "He made love to me," she insisted. "At his place."

"You don't make love with Mason Philips," Cade said with a laugh. "You have mint tea and you have long walks along the river. You hold hands with Mason Philips. You don't make love with a man like that."

"You're so sure," Elizabeth said. "And you're so wrong." She stepped to the side and started for the stairs. Then, at the first step, she had another thought and turned around. Quite seriously, in a hushed voice, she said, "What you and I had is over now. I mean it. And I want you to accept it. This—what just happened—I don't want you to do that again."

"The hell it's over. Not by a long shot."

"Yes," she said firmly, "it is." Her eyes were clear and her voice was steady as she explained. "I haven't told you anything about my situation."

"I don't care about your situation. And your body doesn't seem to care about any situation."

"Listen to me! Hear me, dammit! Financially, I'm in a very bad way."

"I didn't think you took in boarders to keep you company."

"You're so right. There's virtually nothing for me to do to get myself solvent. I may lose everything my family has worked for. Generations of effort all thrown away. But Mason Philips can get me out of this mess. He can save my mill. He wants to marry me."

"And then he gets what you own."

"If that's supposed to hurt, it doesn't. All the hurt's been done already. Now I survive. In spite of what you think, Mr. Delaney—"

"Oh, you can call me Cade. Remember me? The guy in your bed who—"

"Shut up! You're disgusting."

"Sorry. I didn't want to be crude, but since we're being so frank, why not skip all the Southern belle pretense? I know you, Elizabeth Hart. I've slept with you. I know you aren't some wilted flower, in bed or out of it. Fact."

"All right, all right," Elizabeth said, and sighed deeply. Her eyes, which had been glittering with fury a moment before, seemed to retreat deeper into the oval frame of her face. For a moment she remained thoughtful. When she finally spoke again it was without bravado or outrage. Instead, a genuine weariness underscored each word. "I was going to say that I am not a stupid woman—not entirely, that is." She looked directly at Cade. "Maybe the way I've acted with you, you'd think so."

"Why? Because of what happened in bed? Even Southern princesses are entitled to their fair share of lust, just like ordinary folk. It's an inalienable right of all human beings. You should read the Constitution again."

"No," she said, still serious. "Not here. In Greenridge you can't have what you really want, and you can't do what you really feel. I'm titled, but not entitled," she said with an ironic laugh. "I'm part of what people like to call the Southern aristocracy, the last of a dying breed. The rules for us aren't the same." She walked slowly to the stairs and ran her hands along the ending curl of the banister as she continued to speak. "Anyway, like many of my fellow Southern aristocrats, I was not brought up to do anything. I know this may sound incredible to you, but I've spent my life encased in a beautiful pink bubble. Parties and luncheons and some do-good charity work that was more an excuse to waste time than to truly help anyone have been my life. Until my husband died. And the bubble burst. And everything changed."

She looked across to Cade. "I'm flat broke," she confessed. "I've got nothing, no resources, financial or even personal, to fall back on. Frankly, I don't even know who I am anymore. I don't fit in with them— Mason's crowd, my old group—because I'm an embarrassment now. And I don't know how to fend for myself in a place like New York. So, you see, I'm being very realistic when I tart myself up and go out with Mason Philips for dinner and continue to play the role that was handed me when I came into this world. And with you alley-catting around here, it doesn't help my cause. I'd like it if you'd lay off. I'd sincerely appreciate it."

"So you'd really marry him?"

She nodded. "If the figures add up, yes."

"Pretty cold-blooded."

"Yes," she said. She glanced down to the floor, ashamed. "I'm going up to bed. If I have any luck, maybe I'll even sleep for a couple of hours. I can always try counting creditors." Over her shoulder, she called back, "Will you lock the door?"

"Yeah, sure. Keeps out the urban sprawl."

He watched her as she went up the stairs, considering his feelings as they were now. It was hard to hate her and it was hard to love her.

"Elizabeth..."

She looked back.

"The truth... did the two of you...?"

Elizabeth smiled faintly. "You called it right. No, of course I didn't sleep with him."

"But you will someday," Cade conjectured. "If the figures add up."

"If the figures add up, yes. That's one of the few things I've learned since Edward's death. There seems to be a balance sheet to life. Sooner or later you've got to even up the score."

When she had disappeared from view, Cade locked the door, then went into the living room and sat listening to the clock on the mantel tick away. He thought of a bomb's mechanism. When it chimed two, he went slowly up the stairs. Outside Elizabeth's door, he stopped.

Chapter Nine

Cade faced the door boldly, as if it were an enemy he had no way of avoiding. Then, as if in response to his thoughts, the door opened slowly and Elizabeth stood before him in a thin, diaphanous gown. He recognized it as the gown she had worn on the balcony the night he had moved in. She had been beautiful that night; now, close to him, he found her even more desirable.

In the dark, the outline of her body was indistinct, but he had already memorized every curve and fold, and his mind could easily fill in what was lost in the dim light.

"You made a pretty good speech down there," he said, speaking softly. "You had me convinced."

"I meant it. Down there."

"The altitude's changed things?" He looked at her questioningly.

She smiled slightly, with more sadness to her eyes than there was merriment on her lips. "Being a Southern princess has worn thin."

"Or maybe you're feeling alone."

"A little of both," she said. "I didn't realize you were that sensitive to my feelings. I'm surprised. And impressed. Maybe even a little touched."

"Don't be," Cade said. "I'm usually only working on an angle when I appear sensitive." It was meant to be a joke, and then again, it wasn't. She gave him a long studious look, as if figuring out the riddle of what was true about him, but apparently either reached no decision or decided to keep what she thought to herself. At any rate, she was ignoring his warning. That bothered him more than slightly. He had thought to absolve himself from any guilt if he found himself in her bed again. Up to now it had been difficult, but not impossible, to view her as the enemy. But her speech downstairs had skewed things badly. Now she was not just the enemy's daughter and a beautiful woman who had lived a vain and shallow life, but a person who was alive and awake to her emotions and even the sensibilities of others. Under this new perspective, he was treating a good woman badly.

"In other words," he said, trying hard to retrieve his callousness, "I didn't just happen to be hanging around outside your door. I wanted something."

"I didn't just happen to open the door either."

"Fine. Then we both understand each other. We both want something and I trust it's the same thing."

"I made some decisions tonight. I really don't have any choice about Mason. I'm going to go through with the marriage. Eventually. Well, there's the trial over Edward's murder. That'll have to be finished first. I've

got that much time, anyway. But I thought you should
know about my plans.''

"Oh, you're worrying that I could feel used," Cade
joked softly and, stepping forward, drew her back into
the bedroom. He closed the door behind them and
locked it. "Don't worry about it. If it comes to that, a
good cry will wash away my disappointment." He was
joking, but now his humor altered. "I want your body,
not a commitment. You want the same thing. So there's
no problem, is there?"

She did not respond at once. Then she said, "It's not
what you think. Not for me." She appeared nervous
now that they were alone. "I just want to touch. I need
to feel alive one last time. Sounds very melodramatic,
doesn't it?" She turned her head slightly, and even in
the dark Cade could make out the flawless patrician
profile. "I never knew what it could be like before
you," she said, and nodded to the bed. "It wasn't anything like that with Edward. Now I'm thinking that
maybe it would have been better if I had never known
the difference. No," she quickly revised, "I *know* it
would have been better. I might have gone on forever
never missing what I never knew existed. But now I
know. And I want you."

Cade stood motionless, watching as she lifted the
gown's straps from her shoulders and let them fall over
her arms.

"I have to be very careful now," she declared as she
pushed the bodice lower and the material slipped over
her waist, uncovering her breasts. "I have to keep remembering that you're only around here on borrowed
time."

Cade had never seen her look so beautiful and vulnerable before. Tremors ran through his body. His

stomach muscles tightened and flexed and the urge to make love to her was almost more than he could endure. He tried to remember back thirteen years ago, tried to focus his mind on the faces of men snarling like rabid animals, as they dragged his father through town that day, tied to a rope at the back of a pickup truck. He saw his father's torn clothes and bloodied body, and he tried with all the will available to him to remember that Elizabeth Hart's father was the man who had given that order.

"I have to remember," Elizabeth said, "that this is nothing to you and nothing to me. Nothing more than what it is physically." She pushed the filmy material over her hips and for a moment the gown clung to her skin, just above the downy triangle.

Cade found his pulse quickening, and fought a violent impulse to take her there, standing, no preliminaries, no words, but just to have her as she was.

"Because," she went on, dropping the material to the floor, "if I thought it was anything else but pure and simple lust, I think it might completely destroy what life I have." She moved closer to him. "You remind me of that, okay? You remind me, Cade Delaney, that this is all you want and this is all I'm ever going to have." She finished the statement with a wrenching fierceness, and her arms came around his neck.

"Elizabeth..." The name on his lips was more of a short cry than a word. It died as her mouth sought his and he lost himself in her kiss. She had arched into him and the willowy feel of her body in his arms made him weak with desire. She was a satiny form, shimmering in the half-light, sliding sinuously down his body. Like hot licks of flame, her tongue moved against his flesh, her teeth teasing and bringing his heat higher until he doubted he would last past the pleasure of her next touch. He held her still, and she waited, then slowly, sensing his control, she began another journey. On her knees, she moved her face against him and he moaned softly against the pleasure, his hands twining restlessly in her hair.

He lowered her to the floor, and with a single movement took her while it was still possible. Flesh like hot silk, a burning, tingling caldron of swirling liquid bliss, sensation upon sensation, enveloped him. He was lost in every perfumed scent of her body. Entering her was to enter every dream he had ever dared imagine during countless nights over countless years.

Lithe and vulnerable, now under his control, she was made to shiver beneath him. Her body arched to his own tempo, and he drove faster, bringing her closer to the brink with each assured thrust.

"Cade..." she cried, and shuddered, losing the will to resist the pleasure any longer. "Cade!"

And he joined her, calling out her name in a low moan as their bodies slipped into the fire of their union.

They lay in bed afterward, wrapped together. His hand stroked her back lightly. She had placed her hand, along with her head, against his chest. Like skeins of silken thread, her hair fanned out over his darkly tanned skin. The feelings in him, as he held her, were tender and therefore dangerously troubling. He felt like a fool—the trickster tricked by his own methods. He closed his eyes and silently cursed himself and the rest of the world as well.

"You didn't tell me," she said sometime later, breaking the silence. "You promised to remind me."

For a moment, he wasn't sure what she meant. For a while he had allowed himself not to think. He had been feeling, luxuriating in the aftermath of the physical pleasure they had shared. Then, almost immediately, the content of their earlier conversation intruded on the fleeting contentment. He had forgotten everything for a time. Forgotten the ugly past, forgotten the ugly future.

"Elizabeth," he whispered, and drew her over to lie on her back, "some things can never be. No matter how much we want them. And no matter how close to having them we come. They remain elusive, just out of reach. Maybe..." he said, and leaned back against the pillow, examining the ceiling for answers, "that's why we value those things so much. And maybe that's why when we can't have what we love, we have to turn our feelings to hate. Because otherwise it would all be too unbearable." He was speaking more to himself than to her.

"Sorry, I don't understand," she said, and shifted on her side. Leaning onto one elbow, she studied his face. "Okay, you're telling me something, but what?"

"You were talking earlier about survival. Well, this is the same thing. It's a matter of survival."

"You're saying you can't love?"

"No, I can love," Cade replied. "I do love," he said impulsively, and brought her against him, kissing her deeply. When he released her, he turned his head to hide his emotion.

But she brought his chin around, and said, "You meant that just now?"

He sighed. "Elizabeth...don't..."

"But you just said—"

"Forget it. Forget what I said. It doesn't make any real difference what I say or what I feel. The bottom line is the same. I'm not staying here with you."

The sharpness of his statement was like a blow against her, and he saw its force registered on her face. Her pain made his all the worse, and for that he found resentment building, and experienced the free-floating anger that life could be so cruel as to allow the love of one person to preclude the love of another. His father or Elizabeth? What kind of choice was that?

"Okay," she said, her voice small with hurt. She lay down and remained still beside him. He could feel her thoughts and hated himself.

"I'm not going to create a scene," she said. "I knew the score going in, didn't I? I told you I did. So I have nothing to complain about."

"It isn't so simple."

"Tell me," she said, searching his face for answers. "At least tell me so I'll understand. It will make it easier when you're not here anymore."

"I can't explain now."

"But someday... You said now. Does that mean—"

"You'll know, Elizabeth. And when you do, you'll understand." *And you'll hate me. Just as I've hated for so many years. Maybe then you'll understand what I'm feeling right now.* But these were his own private thoughts, and until the whole thing played out, she would have no complete answers to the riddle. It had to be that way.

"What could be so terrible? You're married. You've killed a man. What?"

Cade laughed lightly and bitterly, then harder with a demonic glee. He thought he might lose control, the hilarity of what she had said seemed that great and that tragic. "Yes," he said, still partially convulsed. There were tears in his eyes. Yes, he wanted to tell her, I am married to you in my heart and my mind, and always will be, damn you! And I have killed myself by loving and hating too much.

But finally he came down from his madness, and sober, rooted to the earth plain again, he swung out of the bed and stood before her. "Not literally," he said. "Just consider everything that's happened between us this night as merely a figment of the imagination."

"Then tell me, exactly what is real?" She looked up at him, half resolved and half accusingly.

Cade began to dress, thinking of what he should tell her. Should he be cruel? Or should he be honest? He decided upon a compromise. "Real, is that you are a beautiful passionate woman who is locked up in this hell of a town, and I am a man with passions of his own, who is passing through on his way to somewhere else. And for a time, we are together."

"And then it will all end one day."

"Yes."

"But it won't," she said. "Because when I'm lying in bed with Mason for years and years and years, I will be remembering you. And how it was with us."

He had dressed completely, except for his shoes and socks, which he held in one hand. He put them down on the floor beside the bed as he moved beside her and took her hand and kissed it. "You may not want to, my love."

"Oh, I will. I will," she objected vehemently.

"No. The end hasn't happened yet. Endings create new beginnings that change everything that's gone before."

He got up then and was at the door, when she asked, "Cade, is there someone else? Really. I want to know."

He hesitated. Without turning, he said, "There's something else," and closed the door behind him.

The plans for the new mill, which would put Elizabeth's enterprise out of business, were piled in neat rolls on his desk. In the dark they had the look of swords, ready to wound. They would, too, he thought sadly. They would cut deeply and with lethal results. God, he thought, as he fell fully clothed upon his bed, everyone was going to die in this final battle. Even himself. But there was no way out.

Elizabeth hadn't been particularly surprised when Cade left the house the next morning and did not return that night.

She was having a cup of coffee in the dining room, trying to wake up from a sleepless night, and one of the other boarders was with her when Cade came down the stairs. Although the dining room was opposite the living room, on the other side of the hall, he might have marched past without saying a word, pretending not to see her. But her companion spoke up, brightly issuing a greeting to Cade, along with an invitation that he join them. Cade was therefore trapped into making a detour.

"Good morning," he said, first to Mr. Simms, the boarder. Then his attention moved to her, and she tried to smile. The term "piercing look" came to mind. The eyes were green blades, wounding her. What hurt most was that it was such a clean cut, the look of an honest statement, telling her that nothing had changed since last night. Their connection was severed.

Sleeping together again was not the issue. That might or might not ever happen in the future. But there could never be anything more between them, simply because of who she was and what she had to do in her life, based upon the cards life had dealt her; and from what she could understand, things were the same for him.

At least she no longer felt humiliated for desiring him. That was mutual between them. And last night, in his strange way, he had told her he loved her. She believed him. But it was a love that had no place in his life, nor in hers, either.

"There's coffee on the sideboard," Elizabeth said.

"Thanks, can't." He offered no additional explanation, and looked like he wanted to bolt.

Her heart was pounding. Every time he left the house, she imagined it was for the last time. One day it would be. God, what would she do then?

He was carrying some rolls of paper with him, architectural plans, schematics of some type; she didn't know.

Mr. Simms noticed them, too, and asked, "Whatcha got there? Building a house?"

"Plans," Cade said.

"What for?"

"The future," he quipped, true to form, obviously not intending to say anything more. "I'm off," he said. He gave Elizabeth a short, parting look, the kind men leave when they want to escape an emotional scene they can feel brewing. "Maybe today we'll get some rain. Clouds are moving in."

He left. It didn't rain that night, nor did Cade return.

The second day passed, then the third, and Elizabeth wondered if that last meeting between them might have been their last. Perhaps that was how it was all to happen—how and when she least expected the drama to end. Life, when you really thought about it, actually happened that way. It was impossible to second guess when the really great things and the most horrible events would transpire, or how.

On the fourth day of his absence, she returned home from an afternoon spent with Mason Philips. First they had a long lunch, over which he informed her that the Board of Directors at the bank had insisted he call in the loans Edward had taken out to keep the mill in operation. They would sell the equipment and take their losses as quietly as possible.

Elizabeth wasn't particularly surprised by the news. The threat of such an action being taken had been hanging over her long enough now to seem almost like an already accomplished fact rather than the shocking bit of information it actually was.

"Isn't there anything, anything at all you could do to help me last just a bit longer?" she had pleaded with Mason, knowing full well it was a rhetorical question.

"I'm sorry, Elizabeth." He had looked down at his plate, where a half-eaten piece of cheesecake remained. "The fact is, I can't do anything more. Unless . . ."

"Unless I were to marry you."

"It's the only way that I can buy enough confidence. They know with me they'll be able to count on things being turned around. I have a bit of money personally to throw in, get a new sales staff, order supplies—"

"But I can do that, too! I just need time."

"Elizabeth, when will you face facts?"

"As I see it, there's only one fact, Mason. That I'm a woman."

"You don't have the experience. You're not tough enough to run a business."

"Oh, come on, Mason! I can learn. Plenty of women run businesses." Her mind flew to all the inspiring ar-

ticles in the magazines she had read, about women who
started little cottage industries that grew into multi-
million-dollar enterprises. One woman even did it with
cookies! She wondered if any of them had to listen to
speeches of gloom and doom, and if they had ever felt
like going back home and throwing out the entire rec-
ipe.

"Maybe they do," Mason responded, his voice tight.
"And plenty of them run those businesses into the
ground, too. I've got the statistics. But that doesn't
make a bit of difference. Because you aren't like any of
those women anyway. They're a different breed than
you, Elizabeth. This is what I've been trying to make
you see all along. You've simply lost sight of where your
place is. Edward would not have liked this at all."

"Edward! May I remind you, it's because of him that
my place, Mason, is currently in the poor house!" In a
fury, she started to rise.

Mason clamped his hand over hers. "You were not
raised to say foul words and you were not bred to be at
the head of a company."

"What the hell do you think I am? A damn carrot?
Raised? Homegrown in good soil? Something that has
no right to ever leave the garden patch unless it's to be
eaten?"

"You can marry me, Elizabeth, or you can lose the
mill. I've made my offer," Mason said quietly. "It's up
to you to decide what the future will hold. But I will not
debate with you the whole ridiculous feminine movement for equality and independence. It's all well and
good for discussions over tea with your friends, but
words do not pay the light bill. If you want to go to
Charleston or Philadelphia or someplace else and get a
job typing, that option is always open to you. But if you

remain here, then you'll have to bow to the standards that exist. There are not enough discontents here to lead a revolution. There are only two kinds of women in Greenridge. Those who are well taken care of by their men—as you always have been, and can be in the future—and those who are working to support their families alongside their men, and are too tired and busy to give your crazy notions any thought."

Elizabeth sank back into her chair, knowing Mason's words were certainly true enough. Just as true as the situation existing between her and Cade Delaney. There were wrongs in the world that simply could not be righted and passions that could not be requited. Endurance and forebearance seemed the only way—not a solution, but the only way. "How long do I have?" Elizabeth inquired.

"Two weeks. You've got a couple of weeks."

"You know, Mason, you've never said a word about love in all of this talk about marriage."

Mason looked shocked. "But that goes without saying."

"Naturally. How silly of me. I suppose you'd want children?"

"Yes. I would hope for a family."

Elizabeth's gaze drifted through the room that was the town's only decent restaurant besides that of the Greenridge Inn. There were large potted plants and hanging ferns and chairs covered in a soft green shade of velvet and tablecloths of pink fabric. It was all so subtle, all so politely subdued, so terribly genteel. And she hated it because it lacked verve, lacked the colors of passion.

Passion! Lying on the bed with Cade, bodies covered with the sweat of their lovemaking, that was what she loved. Sex that was brutally honest in its intensity, and making love that was so tender she sometimes felt she could hear the movement of his thoughts, and her whole body was filled with indescribable joy and unbearable sadness. The sweet and sour of life, the heat and the ice, passion!

She looked at Mason. God help her, but she would probably soon be living out her remaining days in pastel shades of feeling.

So on that fourth night of Cade Delaney's absence, she was somewhat resolved to her future. It was as if she had sat through her trial, and the sentence was soon to be pronounced, but there was overwhelming evidence to support a conviction. Acquittal, freedom was an unlikely option.

She was in the living room, making an attempt to go over some financial figures on the mill's operation, when Mr. Simms approached.

"I'm sorry, but I'm going to be leaving," he said. "In two days."

"Yes, well . . . I hope you've been comfortable. And I wish you well." She looked back to her work, but he didn't move away, hovering instead nearby, until she had to ask him if there was something else he wished to say.

His skin had grown particularly rosy, or rather it was pale with splotches of red, and a bead of moisture dotted his hairline. He was smallish and thin and always bore a look of anemia about him. Elizabeth thought at first that he might be seriously ill. He looked disoriented, the way a sickly person appears before some sort of major collapse. Then she realized it was simply that he was incredibly nervous about something.

"It's . . . it's . . . the woman," Mr. Simms finally stuttered. He broke off and waited, as if he expected Elizabeth to continue for him.

"The woman. Yes?" was all she said, and she waited.

"Well, you've seen her then," he said, relief flooding his face.

"Seen? Who am I supposed to have seen?"

"Oh, my. Then you haven't." This was obviously a blow, and he sank into the nearest chair and contemplated his fingers. "I was afraid of that." He looked up, pleading with her. "It's why I'm moving, you see. Because of the woman. I'd been very happy here, but when I started to see her, well, I thought that perhaps I was becoming sick again." He stopped, catching himself in an unwanted exposure. "Anyway, I thought that maybe you had seen her. And then I could stay."

"I'm afraid none of this is making any sense, Mr. Simms. Could you maybe try to explain things a bit more completely? What woman?"

"I saw her outside several times during the past week. From my window, I saw her. Once in the late afternoon and twice—or maybe it was three times? I don't know, I get muddled when these things happen—I saw her at night." He rose and moved to the window, looking out to the front. "She watches," he said. "I'm sure she's watching me."

"Why would a woman want to watch you?" Elizabeth asked, beginning to understand that the woman was in his mind.

"I don't know," he said. "The others used to watch me, too. And I never knew why they came either."

"Others?"

"They didn't really exist."

"Oh, I see. So you just imagined them," Elizabeth said kindly, and was glad he was leaving, although he had been harmless enough and really pleasant in a wimpy sort of way.

"Yes. I finally went to get some help. I went to a hospital where I stayed for a while, and they helped me to understand that sometimes a chemical thing happens in my brain which makes me think that people are out there. I take my medicine, however, and this has not happened for some time. If I take my medicine it never happens, you see. So now this is very upsetting. It means that the medicine is not working and I don't know what to do. I'll have to go back there, to the hospital. If I don't, things may get difficult. Too confusing." He stood up suddenly. "I'm going to go upstairs now. I'm sorry. Really."

Although she was touched by Mr. Simms's predicament, she was glad he would be going. With all the complications in her life at the moment, she didn't need someone else to take care of—she was having enough difficulty looking out for herself.

At eleven, she found her eyes growing heavy and decided to call it a day. She was at the front door almost ready to close it and was idly wondering when Cade's car would reappear, when something in her line of vision moved.

She stood still, at first merely curious to make out what it had been, and then suddenly the first rush of fear traveled her spine. It zipped up her back like a shaft of cold steel, and the impulse radiated icy shocks along every nerve ending in her body. A second before she might have moved from the door. But now the sense of dread paralyzed her and all she could do was stand there in the light of the hall, in clear view of what was out there in the dark that might be watching her even now. Mr. Simms was not crazy.

Chapter Ten

A moment passed and Elizabeth decided that there had been nothing out there after all. The notion that something had moved—had darted away from the large oak closest to the house—was an idea probably put in place by Mr. Simms.

The flood of fear abated, and her heart, which had been thumping in huge leaps, finally began to quiet. There was still that peculiar tingling from the adrenaline, but she felt in control of her body again, and was about to close the front door when the thick covering of clouds broke overhead. In a stream of moonlight, the pale, silvered outline of a person rushing alongside the drive to the main road, was clearly visible.

Elizabeth slammed the door closed and locked it. Then she rushed to the back, and made certain that door was also secure. But the windows were open in the living room, and screens would be nothing to tear apart if someone wanted to break into the house. She dashed back down the hall to the front.

Switching off the lights in the living room, she ran quickly to the bank of large windows. She felt as if she were in a glass fishbowl. How long had she been observed? How many nights? And who would want to do such a thing? She had just tugged the first window down when a flashing light changed the direction of her thoughts.

A car had turned into the drive. In a panic, she slammed each of the other windows shut. The last one had just been locked when the car pulled to a stop and she saw it was Cade.

He was by the car door, leaning in and still engaged in gathering his things, when she burst into the night, calling his name. He turned in surprise.

"Oh, God...I'm so glad it's you...that you're back...oh God..." she cried and rushed against him, her arms taking a stranglehold around his neck. She was shaking from fear, and there were hot tears running down her face that he brushed away as he held her from him.

"What's happened?" he asked, holding both her arms to keep her from jittering. "Hey, easy...it's okay. Tell me."

"There's someone out there," Elizabeth said wildly.

Cade turned his head to where she had looked down the drive. It was empty.

"Who?"

"I don't know," she whispered, as if they might be watched even then.

"Come on," Cade said. He gathered his things in one arm and led her, with the other arm around her waist, to the house.

After they were inside, and she had made a special point of locking the door and testing it twice, she joined Cade in the living room. He was putting on a light, but she leaped forward with alarm. "No, don't."

"Elizabeth," Cade said, bemused by her paranoia. "Tell me what the hell's happening around here?"

Elizabeth moved to one of the windows, and peering out from the side, said, "Mr. Simms told me tonight that he's seen a woman watching the house. Several times. But he's had this before, so he thought maybe he was having one of his delusions. But then I saw someone, too."

"You don't think you might have—"

"No. I saw someone. It wasn't my imagination. He, she... whoever... was standing by the oak tree there, the closest one, watching me."

"And you think it was a woman?"

"Maybe. I don't know. It only just happened. Did you see anyone? They would have been running up the road."

Cade shook his head. "No, nothing."

"I don't understand why," she said, staring at the floor in perplexity. Then she looked up. "It isn't someone for you, is it?"

"No," he answered, and smiled. "I haven't any wronged women in my past. Maybe Mr. Simms has."

Elizabeth laughed slightly. "Mr. Simms? I doubt if he's had any women, wronged or otherwise in his life. Other than the imaginary ones."

"Tomorrow you call the police," he said. "Tonight you stay with me."

"Do you think it's so dangerous?"

"No," he said. "But I want you with me anyway."

So it was like that, a simple decision, totally natural, that she was to stay with him. It was clearly unexpected for both of them that they should have walked together up the stairs, a feeling of closeness filling the slight gap between their bodies, and entered his room.

"You lied to me," Elizabeth said, when she was secure in his bed. "Down there."

He turned, his expression befuddled. "I generally remember my sins. Tell me," he said, "this one must have slipped past."

"You do think it's dangerous for me." Elizabeth searched his face for what he may or may not have been willing to admit.

"I don't know. It might be nothing at all. Anyway, you were afraid."

She nestled closer to him. "I'm not anymore."

"Elizabeth—"

"No, don't," she said, and quickly touched her finger to his lips. "No speeches tonight. I know all of them already. My own, and yours. We both have our destinies outlined for us. Mason for me...and leaving Greenridge one day for you. Let's not spoil this. Tonight," she said laughing, "we were given an unexpected gift. A mysterious woman who provided us with an excuse to be together."

He kissed her softly then, lying half over her. She had been so frightened before that the usual sensation of lust that arose whenever they were together, had for once not overwhelmed her senses. But now the heat arose again, and she was easily accessible as he moved completely atop her. The first time they made love it was with the same urgency as always, but the second time, which came after she had almost drifted to sleep, he took her with a gentleness that was exquisite, and in many ways even more erotic than his more forceful possession of her body had been.

They awoke together the following morning. There was a sweetness between them that had been absent in their relationship before. Yet she was under no illusion that whatever they were experiencing together would last.

She was still in his bed, when he came out of the shower and began to dress. He was the most beautiful man she had ever seen, and as she observed him moving about the room in nothing but his shorts, a wave of sadness swept over her with a paralyzing force. She could almost hear the sands of their time together slipping through an hourglass. Rashly, she even thought that she might get herself pregnant! But knowing Cade, it wouldn't matter. He would look upon her stupidity as the trick it was, and although he might very well support the child, he would never let such a time-worn cliché bond them together.

While he had dressed, he appeared as lost in his own thoughts as she was in hers. Finished at last, he came over and sat on the edge of the bed. With a certain amount of relief she noted he had not put on one of his more formal outfits, which meant he wouldn't be going on one of his mysterious trips which would keep him away for a few days. He wore a tan cotton shirt, the kind that looks better wrinkled, as if it were designed to be worn by foreign war correspondents, or by daring men who went on safari in dark continents. His jeans were a light blue and faded. They hugged his body easily, like a second skin, as he moved with a fluid animal grace, unconscious of the physical perfection that was a natural part of him. She had to admit, Greenridge hardly constituted the right terrain for the image he represented.

It was as if he had somehow gotten off course and had landed temporarily in this mundane circumstance. She could imagine him one day, somewhere else where he better belonged, with more exciting people, mentioning his brief sojourn in Greenridge. It would undoubtedly be a fleeting account, preceded by a slight laugh: "Oh, yes. I spent an odd couple of months in this little town. What was it called? Well, anyway, it doesn't matter." He was everything to her. He had changed the very core of her being, and to him she would not matter.

But looking down at her now, he sat for a moment with his eyes serious, and she could tell he was choosing his words with caution. Again that familiar feeling of leaden inevitability took over. He would be telling her he was leaving for good in a couple of days, a couple of hours—what difference did it make? It was going to happen eventually.

"What will you be doing today?" he asked her.

"What?" The question was so far removed from what she had been expecting, she could only laugh. It was so ordinary, so sweetly domestic, so totally foreign to any dialogue that had passed between them in the past, that in the next moment she was forced to reconsider the statement's face value. Something more than polite, idle curiosity had prompted his interest in her day's schedule.

"Your plans," he asked again. "What are they?"

"I'd thought of going to the mill." She sighed, thinking of the gloom awaiting her there. "Why?"

"I just wondered," he said, seeming slightly relieved.

"For a purpose," she returned. "You're worried about something."

He looked away. "No. Not worried really. But that woman last night ... It's strange, that's all."

"She's probably someone out of Mr. Simms's past. Maybe he'd been involved with some woman who just couldn't stay away."

"Just be careful, okay? You're mostly alone here during the days."

"You know," Elizabeth said, relaxing against the pillows, "you actually sound like you care about what happens to me."

"Sure I do. You've got a great body. You think I want to lose my creature comforts?" He kissed her, and made it possible for her to pretend what he had said was only a joke.

"You'll be back tonight?"

"If you make it worth my while," he said, grinning, and rose from the bed.

"You Yankee carpetbaggers sure have a lot of nerve."

"Yup, we're total opportunists." He was at the door, and turned. "Don't ever forget that, love."

"You're not joking, are you?"

"No," Cade said solemnly enough to erase any doubt. "I'm not."

He left her then, left her with the usual contradictory feelings of hope and despair. As he gave with one glance, he took away with the next word.

The east side of Greenridge was divided neatly from the west side by railroad tracks. Cade knew this other part of town well. It was a different world from that inhabited by the descendants of the great landowners. For a while after the Civil War, it had served as a shanty town for former slaves disoriented and struggling to make sense out of their new freedom. Later, it became Cracker Land, as the rich kids of Greenridge called it amongst themselves. It was a place where migrant farm workers would stay during part of the season, and where the more stable community of blue collar workers would call home the full year round. Until thirteen years ago, it had been home to him.

The car gave a slight shudder as it made the crossing over the rails. To Cade it was like going back in time.

He drove a way down the main road, lined on both sides by cotton fields, then took a right turn which led to the colony of small working class shack houses scattered within a two or three-mile radius.

Nothing had changed since he'd left. If anything, the area looked worse to him. He didn't know if this was because it really was more run down, or if this impression was due to an expanded perspective.

There was a business center of sorts, consisting of a general store with a couple of gas pumps in front, a post office about the size of a good-sized closet, a barber shop, and a feed shop. Once there had been a restaurant, but that was boarded up now. The road running through this dilapidated scene was ostensibly blacktop, however a proliferation of potholes and huge fissures, gave it the appearance of a lunar landscape. The area's one saving charm was the trees. Large trees of various types dotted the land, creating interesting flickering patterns of sunlight on the ground.

Cade parked the car off to the side of the general store. He got out and stood a while in the heat, looking around for signs of life. It was absolutely still with not even a hint of a breeze enlivening the mid-morning climate.

Finally, he walked across the dirt parking area, and into the main building. The screen door whined open, and whined closed, with an extra little snap at the end.

"Mornin'" he said to the proprietor.

The man, who was passing the end of middle age, nodded. A fan beside him twisted and whirred in Cade's direction.

"Got anything cool?"

"Over there," the man said, nodding to a free-standing cooler.

Cade slid the plastic covering to the side and dug into the pit, extracting a diet drink. He paid for it silently, sensing that his best course was to back off and not appear too eager to make friends.

"Where you from?" the man asked.

"New York."

"Long way outta your neighborhood."

"Yeah. Things are real different here."

"Not much goes on, I guess. Not like in New York."

"Won't hear me complain. Muggings, murders..."

"Even had one here," the proprietor said with a strange note of pride.

"Not here! Here? Really?"

"Few months ago. Man killed one of the leading citizens. Going to court for it, too."

"Incredible," Cade said, and shook his head. "What reason would anyone have around here to kill someone else? Unless it was over a woman." He laughed, the way men do when they commiserate over the differences between the sexes.

"Weren't no woman. Roy Buck just got mad. Killed his boss, owner of the textile mill. Buck got laid off a while before. Thought he'd get even, I guess. Anyway,

Roy Buck was pretty crazy. They'll right likely just put him out to pasture in the crazy farm.''

"Must have made a mess of a lot of people's lives," Cade said, closing in for his own kill.

"Yup, rightly did, I suppose. Left a widow—the wife of the man got killed."

"What about the other guy's family?"

"Wasn't married. Only had a sister. Elva's got some kids. Roy used to support them all up to the time he got laid off. Well, Elva'll be leaving in just a bit down the line. Already started packing. See them boxes there?"

Cade looked. Four or five cartons were stacked together in the corner.

"Every time I get an empty box, I just leave it for her, and she uses 'em to pack up in."

"Well," Cade said, backing away, "think I'll walk the kinks out of my legs a little before taking off."

In a mere ten minutes, the sun seemed to have doubled in its intensity. The air hung close around him. Heat waves created strange wobbling mirages in the near distance and beneath him, blisters of tar were forming on the road's surface. Above, the huge white clouds looked immobile, yet mysteriously continued to build higher, ever higher. A few crows came fluttering down and sat watching him on a broken line of barbed wire running the length of the road. He walked on.

It was eerily quiet, and he wondered if that was because everyone had jobs, or if the residents had picked up stakes—as Elva Buck was soon to do—and left Greenridge for, ironically, greener pastures. Looking at the houses, it was impossible to tell what the situation might be. Two or three of the dwellings he had passed were closed up—against the heat, or because of vacancy? A fourth house had old pieces of cars strewn in the front and back, torn curtains on the windows, and wash limp on a line on the side, and yet not a sound emanated from the property.

Suddenly, Cade heard a shout off to the side.

He turned, just in time to see a boy in shorts and no shoes break a switch over a mangy dog's back. The dog ran, or rather limped, full speed ahead trying to evade its persecutor. "Come 'ere, Tag...come 'ere boy. I won't do it again. Come on, Tag," the boy cajoled slyly.

The dog had jittered up beside Cade, and was darting back and forth from his heels, sniffing and panting.

"Hi," the boy said, hanging back a little, suspicious of Cade. "That's my dog."

"How come you're hitting him then?" Cade asked. The boy was about eight and as skinny as the dog. He had a dirty face, dirty body, and his hair was cut short in a home style attempt at a flat top. There were scabs on the side of his head where a bug had gone to work. Cade didn't know if he felt more saddened or angry, or just plain revolted.

"Don't know," the boy said.

"Don't you think it hurts?" Cade asked.

"Don't know," the boy said. He backed off, not wanting to continue the conversation.

"Do you know where Elva Buck lives?"

The boy nodded and pointed. "Down there."

"Thanks," Cade said, and handed the boy a dollar. "Ice cream goes good on a day like this." He dug into his pocket and retrieved some change, enough to buy a dog biscuit or soup bone. "Something for your friend, too."

The boy scampered ahead, with the dog racing along beside him. Cade moved on, going in the direction of the Buck residence.

The house was off the side of the road, down a small ravine. There were a few large trees giving shade, and a dry creek behind the frame dwelling. The paint was peeling and the screens were torn. Once it had looked very different; once it had a fresh coat of paint and the screens were in place and the creek had been full. Once it had been his home. Strangely, he was not beset by nostalgia. What he had come to accomplish took precedence in his mind.

As Cade approached the front porch, he made out the drawn curtains and front door closed against the heat. Knocking, he waited and got no response. He knocked again, and finally turned and started away, going several yards as if to give the impression of leaving; then suddenly, unexpectedly, he turned back.

He was being watched. A curtain fluttered and stealthy fingers drew out of sight as he stared back at the house.

Ten minutes later, he was seated on a frayed sofa, speaking with Elva Buck. He guessed she was near his age, but at first glance would have appeared far older. Her hair was a dull dishwater blond, barely shoulder length and worn twisted into a rubber band. Limpid blue eyes seemed to dissolve into her pale skin. She was a woman without any definition in color or personality. As tattered as her surroundings, she appeared drained by more than the heat.

"I guess maybe it's changed since you lived here," she was saying. She had just apologized for not having anything to offer him by way of refreshments. Her children had gone to stay with a sister in Charleston, she told him. She would soon be leaving also. "I only have to wait for the—"

She didn't want to talk about the trial and Cade knew it wouldn't be any good to push her. Instead, he asked her other questions—things about the town, about the mill, about where she would be going and what she would be doing, and everything he learned made him nervous, namely because she seemed so nervous.

"I heard about your father," she said. "He was a good man. We came after, but we heard he tried to stand up to them. But they got him in the end. And he had to leave town, too."

"You mean, you have to leave town?" Cade asked.

"No," she laughed. "I'm nobody special like your father. I'm not anyone. I just don't have a thing for me now that Roy's gone. No place to work, really. The mill's all but closed."

"What if there was another mill," Cade asked.

"There isn't," she said.

"But what if there was? What if I were to open another mill and I would hire you? Would you stay then?"

Her face went white. "No," she said.

"You'd still leave."

"Yes," she whispered.

"Are you afraid of something, Elva?" Cade pressed.

"You'd better go. Nothing personal," she said. "But you'd better go now."

"Did your brother really hate Edward Hart enough to kill him?"

"You'd better go," she repeated.

"Elva?"

Her eyes grew cloudy. "Roy was crazy. He didn't know what he was doing. He just went crazy, that's all. I'm sorry, you better go."

It was past noon by the time Cade made it back to his car. The heat was like a branding iron coming down on his head, and inside the car would be the cool blast of air conditioning. Yet he stayed where he was, needing that moment to gather the past back and refuel his present with the determination to proceed on his course.

Seeing Elva Buck had both reminded and shaken him. He had come back from the city, more clever and far richer than he had ever dreamed he could become when he had lived in the house now belonging to Elva. He felt like a knight returning to his kingdom to fight the sleeping dragon that appeared every so often to devour and plunder the countryside. But away, on his long journeys, he had forgotten that beast's power and ugliness; now, once again, he found himself trembling in its very real presence.

He no longer could see Elizabeth solely as the enemy; she was really a dragon's pawn. Mason Philips was capable of devouring Elizabeth in a blast of red fire if she did not go along with his plans. It was not what Elva Buck had said that told him as much, but what she had been afraid to tell him. There was something ugly going on in Greenridge, something frightening and dangerous.

Once long ago the dragon had risen against his father. Cade stood in the street and stared down a tunnel of the past. His father had been one of the hundreds of workers who had been paid paltry wages at the mill, while Elizabeth's father had amassed an ever greater fortune. When union organizers came into town, his father had agreed to spearhead the movement that would ensure safe working practices and decent wages to live on. The town's old guard fought an all-out war of physical terrorism and financial intimidation against those people who initially joined forces with his father. The union organizers thought better of their initial plan to enter Greenridge, deciding to concentrate their efforts in a less insular environment.

So his father lost his job. Fueled by righteousness, he purchased the small factory with his life's savings and money from his wife's insurance policy. He offered fair wages and a share in the profits to any who would work for him. Many men came, grateful for the alternative. But then the ugliness began.

Houses of workers were burned to the ground; a child was run over and left crippled; mothers could no longer afford the prices of groceries, raised by local merchants as added pressure.

His father set up a rally in the town to protest the violence and opposition to free enterprise. Late that afternoon, a group of men with hoods over their faces came to their small home—the one which Elva Buck now occupied. They took his father and dragged him through the town tied to the back of a truck. At the same time, another band of Greenridge's finest set a fire at the factory in which two men died. The price to pay was too dear for supporters after that. Cade and his father did the only thing they could; they took the train out of town. The dragon had won.

Standing in the heat, Cade reviewed the disparate facts which were not now as unrelated as they once had been. Edward Hart was dead. Elizabeth Hart had a factory that was being foreclosed upon. Roy Buck was being tried for a murder which everyone saw him commit. And his sister Elva was very evasive and for some unknown reason also very frightened. The one link to everything was the mill. And the one person who controlled the current destiny of the mill was Mason Philips.

Mason Philips, thought Cade, as he slipped into the driver's seat, was worth a consideration or two or three.

Chapter Eleven

Mason had just returned from a pleasant lunch with two of his friends at the Greenridge Country Club. Everything, it seemed, was finally coming together in precisely the way he had planned. It was just a matter of time before Elizabeth would agree to marry him, and after that he would have the funds to prolong the mill's operation and turn the whole enterprise around. This would make him look very good, very good indeed.

But even all this, although commendable, did not constitute the summit of his vision. Elizabeth and the mill merely reflected the groundwork for what was to come after. With Elizabeth by his side he would have secured a fine blue-blood American pedigree to flaunt in the right high places as a reflection of his own worth. Likewise, her mill would provide him with a backdrop representing substantial physical security. Along with these credentials, he would bring his own sterling record as a banker to the starting gate of the gubernatorial race.

And later down the road, there would be the bid for the presidency. At the thought, a vague thrill traveled through Mason. The notion of being president of the United States had never seemed farfetched to him. Other presidents had come out of backwater towns and changed the history of the nation. He could easily envision his own name added to that esteemed list of patriots.

After lunch, he began his afternoon in his usual manner, returning calls and intermittently touching base with those citizens whose names he kept listed on a special file used for social networking. As with everything else in his life, he was methodical in maintaining his relationships. He would contact each person in strict rotational order. The time of the month for reestablishing the connection was always moved forward, so as not to appear premeditated. Through this means he was able to garner valuable scraps of information from people with whom he ordinarily would never have association. The range of news he received was well worth the social slumming endured.

This afternoon he dialed Rupert Blackthorn, the proprietor of the general store in the area of town occupied by the lower echelon. Mason could always count on Rupert as a veritable wellspring of trifling data. It never failed that something interesting came out of their chats. This day was no exception.

Mason sat forward on his chair. His finger gripped the phone more tightly as he waited for Rupert to repeat what he had just said.

"Man came by. Said he was from New York. Went down the road and visited with Elva Buck."

Mason already knew it had to be Cade Delaney, but made Rupert describe the man just for the sake of certainty. It had to be Delaney. From the very first, he had sensed the man was trouble.

"What did he talk to Elva for?" Mason responded with a rasp. His throat had gone suddenly dry. "What would a man from New York want with Elva Buck?"

"Don't know," Blackthorn answered slowly. Being the repository of what was obviously turning out to be inflammatory information made him cautious. "Elva didn't say nothin'. Just looked at me blank when she came in to buy bread and I asked her. I told her straight I saw him going down to her place. But she didn't have nothing to say."

"Okay," Mason snapped. "What else is new over there, Rupert?"

"Well, Jerry Bear's got a good melon crop this year, 'spite of the drought . . ."

Rupert droned on, but Mason was no longer listening. His mind was careening about on a hysterical rampage. Cade Delaney was going to be some kind of trouble to him unless he acted fast, Mason thought, forever astute to any roadblocks in his path. He had made a previous mental note to investigate Elizabeth's boarder further, but now he moved that matter up the list to his top priority. He had thought of Delaney in terms of being a romantic threat, but now this was something else entirely. Talking to Elva Buck! It had to be stopped.

Once he formulated the plan, Mason got off the phone fast. He told his secretary he had to go off on an urgent matter and to cancel his two afternoon appointments. By the time he climbed into his Cadillac, he was sweating like a chain-gang road worker.

Twenty minutes later he stood in the tiny dark living room of Elva Buck.

"Now, Elva . . . we had an understanding, you and I. Didn't we, Elva? Isn't that what we had? So what is this business I've been hearing about you opening your mouth to this man from out of town?"

Elva looked down, her expression sullen. "I didn't say anything."

"Well, that's real fine, Elva. I'm pleased to hear that. But what I want now is that you say something to me. Elva, what did Cade Delaney have to say to you today?"

Elva shrugged. She glanced briefly up from the floor, a flash of defiance appearing briefly in her eyes before she looked off to the side and said, "He was just asking about the town."

"The town?"

"He didn't know where some of the roads led."

"Why, Elva, would a man you don't even know stop by your house and ask about roads? Are you some kind of authority on the byways of this town? If you are, Elva, I have never known that. And I have always made it a point to know a great, great deal about what goes on in these parts." Mason moved forward. Elva took several steps back, maintaining their distance.

"He thought because I lived here . . ."

"Oh, stop, stop!" Mason waved his arm, dismissing her claim. He spoke sharply. "Do you like our arrangement, Elva?"

She eyed him stonily. In a whisper, she said, "My kids need the money."

"That's right. So it wouldn't be too smart for you to say the wrong thing to someone." Elva only stared. He knew she would never tell him anything about anything. He could ask her the time of day and she would either lie or keep her mouth clamped shut. There was something about her that Mason found aggravating to the extreme. It was that infernal blankness, that ignorant unwillingness to capitulate to his obvious power over her. A rage had been simmering in him for a long while, certainly ever since he had heard the disturbing news that afternoon about Delaney snooping about, and now Elva's expressionless face drew out the fury in its full measure.

Mason's hand shot out unexpectedly, making contact with a smacking sound. Elva listed off to the side, her eyes instantly filling, but she made no sound of protest.

Five minutes later Mason climbed back into the Cadillac. He straightened himself in the rearview mirror, taking care to smooth back his hair, tuck his shirt in neatly, and make himself appear the presentable, upstanding citizen again. What had happened with Elva Buck had been simply unavoidable and he suffered no remorse. He had always done what was most expedient when it came to meeting a goal; right or wrong had nothing to do with the method of accomplishment.

His ministrations completed, his attention wandered from the mirror to the view outside. He had been so preoccupied with his thoughts, he hadn't noticed the change in the external world. A strange stillness had settled over the landscape. The late afternoon had grown prematurely dark, the sun totally eclipsed by a dense layer of clouds. If violence had a color, it would be that of the heavens now—grays and deep purples, pulsating yellow-green fringes, the stain of magenta bleeding through the center. If violence had a voice, it would be soft like the air about him now. It would be no more than a whisper beneath the eerie quiet.

Mason stared up through the windshield. Something bad was going on up there. Something had been gathering all summer, just waiting, and now it was going to finally happen. Then he looked back to the little shack of a dwelling occupied by Elva Buck. She had just damn well better keep her trap shut.

It was the early part of the evening. Elizabeth stood on the balcony of her bedroom, looking out over an expanse of property that had belonged to her family for generations. As of this day, the status of her inherited land holdings was going to change. That afternoon, she had spent the better part of three hours with the plant manager and a gray-suited man from Chicago who represented the end of that once glorious past. The deal she had hammered out would at least buy her a slice of the future. For how long she didn't know, but time was now a valuable commodity for her and she was willing to pay almost any price to own it.

She glanced back into her room. The clock on her nightstand read almost five. A small leap of excitement passed through her. She hoped Cade would be home soon.

Home soon! What a harmonious domestic ring the phrase presented. Once such words had represented reality in her life—waiting for Edward to return from the mill and sit opposite her at the dinner table where they would be served lovely meals by deferential servants. Well, that was all gone now, along with so much else.

Nevertheless, there was something enormously comforting in knowing, for once, that she could expect to hear the sound of Cade's engine coming up the drive, rather than having to sit there on pins and needles all night, waiting and wondering if he would be making one of his irregular appearances. In a life where so little was special, Cade represented a great deal. But he would anyway, she knew, no matter what was going on. Cade was a once-in-a-lifetime man.

She had the news to share with him, and could hardly wait. Rather than feeling sad over relinquishing property that had once seemed as much a part of her as her arms or legs, she felt clever and strong. She was surviving. She wasn't just going down without a fight; whatever happened she would have at least splashed about and created some waves. That was something; no, that was a lot. Maybe there was a bit of her ancestors' old fight in her after all.

Inside the house it was stifling, close to unbearable. Even outside on the balcony, it was hardly any better. The air had reached an all-time heaviness. Everything her eyes touched seemed coated in a peculiar yellow-green light reflected from the clouds blocking the sun. All afternoon, the billowing monster forms had been changing, slowly at first as they had done every afternoon since summer began.

Periodically, Elizabeth would glance to the window and see that peaks and craters had formed where before there had only been the predictable bulbous shapes. Edges like jagged teeth grew out of formerly flat surfaces. And all the while the colors kept changing. The blanket overhead was now a dark bruise, hell's colors bleeding through the sky. There would be a storm for certain that night. All season they had waited for this time of relief, thinking it would be sweet. But no gentle Indian summer's rain would come out of that sky this night, Elizabeth thought. Tonight the devil would ride roughshod over the parched land.

She bathed and changed into a cool white cotton dress. The material, from India—a country that knew everything there was to know about heat—was so thin as to be almost indecently transparent. As there were no roomers about that night, she decided to be reckless. Other than the silk lace panties, which did not show beneath the folds of the circular skirt, she wore no other undergarments. At certain angles the outline of her breasts were clearly visible beneath the loose, scooped neckline. But she didn't care about maintaining the old rigid code of propriety that had characterized her former life. She felt free and sensual, and it seemed completely right that she express her newly evolved nature.

But besides this deliberate bent for self-expression, she also embraced comfort. Her hair was scooped up high to her crown and clasped securely. Even so, heavy silvery strands found their way to the sides of her face and along the nape of her neck, and as she passed a mirror she knew the state of semidisarray also illuminated the emerging personality within. She might have stepped from a time machine, a serving wench at a country inn. If tomorrow night, she was something else, someone else, that would be all right, too. Life was suddenly becoming an exhilarating adventure.

Two hours later she greeted Cade effusively in the downstair's hall.

"Good, you're home!" She could not resist using the phrase, nor could she resist kissing him.

He did not object. The kiss lengthened into a more serious encounter. She felt him harden and pulse against her. His hand roamed along the small of her back and farther down over the sweep of hip and buttock.

"Come on," he said, and broke away with the clear intention of leading her up the stairs to bed.

She would have liked to have followed, but instead said, "Later. For dessert. I've made dinner for us," she announced gaily. "Oh, and before I forget..." She grabbed a piece of mail from the long, narrow hall table. Handing it to him, she said, "It came by special messenger today."

As she spoke, he turned the envelope over in his hand, not opening it, but studying it intently as if he could see through to the contents. Whatever the inside message, he did not look particularly pleased. But she was high enough that his gloom did not diminish her good spirits.

"It so happens we're alone tonight. The others have miraculously all found something to do at the same time. None of them will be lurking about, so we can get as crazy as we'd like. Maybe spit watermelon pits at the moon! Oh," she added as an afterthought, "and Mr. Simms has packed his bag and cleared out for good."

It was only then that Cade seemed in touch with her conversation. "The woman—there wasn't any more trouble?"

"No," Elizabeth said. "First of all, I wasn't even here until late this afternoon. And besides, I think the whole matter should be dropped. The woman was probably some stray out of Simms's past, and now that he's run off she won't be back again."

Cade let the matter go, and for that she was glad. She was feeling good for a change. There had been enough doom in her life that summer to last many a year. Things were turning around for her at last.

A distant grumble of thunder, like a giant's drum roll, made her look apprehensively past Cade. Beyond the screen door the sky flashed brilliantly, then became quiet again.

They exchanged looks. "Maybe this one won't pass over." Elizabeth looked to the window. "And it looks like it could get ugly."

"I'm sure it will," he said. For a moment he remained silent, his eyes seemingly focused on the natural forces assembling on the horizon. But a passing shadow of sadness swept his face, and as always Elizabeth wondered at the secrets hidden behind the facade of emotional reserve. "No," he said, at last turning back to her, "we haven't a chance in hell of this passing."

He was staring at her with that peculiar intensity she could never fathom. It wasn't the first time she felt he was speaking on several levels at once.

She might have even said something, but before she could form a safe context in which to broach the subject, Cade excused himself to wash and change into something fresh before dining, and the moment was lost.

A few minutes later he rejoined her downstairs. She heard his footsteps in the dining room.

"You can open the wine, please!" Elizabeth called from inside the kitchen, her voice cutting through the extreme silence.

As there were so few sounds, the slightest noise seemed magnified out of proportion. The windows were open wide to the night, but not even the frogs or crickets were stirring.

She came back into the dining room, carrying three serving dishes of food on a large tray. His mood had not altered from when he had left. She did not know if her impression of strained expectancy was caused by the dense atmosphere, or by the tension she picked up from Cade's manner, but she was unwilling to succumb to the psychic discomfort generated by either. Instead she concentrated on uplifting the energy.

"Hope you're hungry. I think I made enough for the whole Italian army." She placed each bowl on the table and looked down at her gastronomical accomplishments with a degree of domestic satisfaction she hadn't experienced in a long time.

"Oh," she said, "one more thing!" She traveled across the room to an antique sideboard and pulled out a book of matches. "The finishing touch," she proclaimed, striking a flame.

She had thought several times about the candles, and in the end decided to go all the way and include them in the evening. They were red tapers, graceful and festive, and after lighting them she sat down and admired the finished setting she had created. "The only line I drew was in the violin music. I thought that might be overkill." She waited for him to laugh.

The laugh didn't come. He was lost in some other world, a place that was obviously a million light years away, judging by the look on his face. His lack of reaction was disappointing. She had really looked forward to sharing this evening—everything—from food to atmosphere to news.

She passed him the bowl of cold pasta salad. "Was it the letter?"

His eyes met hers briefly, as if surprised by the insight. But he did not reply. Instead, he countered by adopting an obvious forced interest in her domestic efforts. "I'm impressed. And baffled. When did you find the time for all of this?"

"It didn't take long. Besides, I had a good day. I find myself suddenly energized. I can leap tall buildings and fly faster than a speeding bullet. Boiling noodles was a snap compared to racing freight trains on foot."

Cade finally smiled. He hitched his head toward the window. "Must be all the negative ions."

"Uh-uh," she protested. "Only positive vibes tonight. And they're going to last. This is special," she said, hoisting the bottle of Chablis. She leaned forward to fill their glasses.

"A good year?" he asked, misunderstanding.

"A good day," she corrected.

"Ah, I see. We are speaking of the woman and not the wine."

"You are."

"Am I going to be apprised of the nature of this celebration?"

"Well, if you lift your glass, perhaps I'll make a toast to the occasion and the happy secret will be formally presented."

Cade took up his glass.

"This is goodbye to the past," Elizabeth said, raising the cut crystal, "and hello to the new and glorious future which I have this day assured by way of selling two-thirds of all my properties."

Cade frowned. He did not drink, but merely stared.

Elizabeth sipped from her glass, and looking over the rim of cut crystal, smiled. "It's okay. Really. I'm actually quite happy about it." Still he said nothing, and she finally relented and told the story straight out.

"I can't take full credit for the idea, of course. It was my plant manager who made all the arrangements. An act of desperation, I'm sure, to save his own skin by saving mine. He contacted a big sub-developer who goes around buying up land where housing is scarce. The firm builds cheap houses fast, and then gets out even faster. My manager convinced him that one of the problems with getting people to work at the mill was lack of affordable housing. It's true of course. But the best part is that the sale of the land is going to give me enough cash to hang in with the mill. I'll still have a chance to save it, Cade!''

Now that he knew the whole story, she waited expectantly for his praise. It was not forthcoming. Instead, he merely stared at her with an incredulous expression.

"Cade? It's not the end of the world. It's the beginning of a whole new . . . well, a beginning for me!''

"It's the most stupid thing I've ever heard," he said, and put his napkin down. He rose then. He was halfway to the door when she too leaped from her chair and accosted him before he could entirely escape.

She stood before him, furious and bewildered. "Stupid? You call saving my mill stupid?''

"You can't possibly save that mill. You don't have the knowledge and you don't have the experience—''

"And I'm only a woman," she finished. "Is that what you were going to say?''

"Just let it go, Elizabeth. Make your plans, live your life, but don't include me in your triumphs or your failures.''

"I'm not *including* you. I was merely telling you. As a friend. I wasn't asking for an investment." She was angry. "Well, maybe I was. An emotional investment. Maybe fifteen seconds of, 'What a brave and clever girl you are, my dear!' But I guess that was asking too much of you.''

"We had an understanding." His eyes were fiery with rage. "Our lives are separate. We do not bleed for each other."

"Why," she shot back, "do you always do this to me?"

He was trying to get away from her, but she stepped in front of him again, blocking his path. "This morning you were so concerned. You were—"

"I was having sex with you."

"No," she said, "no . . . this time I know better. This time that's not going to work with me. Because I may not know much about you, but I know when you are feeling something genuine. I feel it, Cade. You can pretend all you want that I'm good for nothing but—"

"Shut up," he said.

"No, I won't. I won't back down or shut up or go away or talk like a nice little girl. I'm a woman. I may not be the most experienced or worldly, but I'm becoming a woman—more and more with every day. And I'm not going back to being what and who I was."

"That has nothing to do with me." A covering of frost seemed to have settled over his eyes. Beneath the coldness, a green fire glowed. "Your psychological development is your business, not mine. I rent a room from you and sometimes when it feels good for the both of us, we sleep together. But eventually I'm going to walk out of that door, and I don't want to have any heart strings trailing from my heels. That's not my scene."

"You care about me," she said, but less with conviction now than with hope that she was not mistaken. There was so much she had not learned yet in life. Perhaps what she felt she knew, she did not really understand after all. Maybe he was telling her the whole, complete truth as it really was. She wondered how many magazines she'd have to read on the dating game, the mating game, the game of breaking up and making up, before she would have all the pieces put together and could make sense out of this crazy new world into which she had been so rudely dropped.

But a part of her already knew the answer to the question. There were no ultimate rules in life. You could only go by what you, individually felt was right for you. And right now she felt like crying. She felt like hitting the man standing before her, because it could all be so different, so good between them if he would just allow it to be. How could they be so close and so far apart? It was a terrible trick of space, like an emotional optical illusion.

Even as she thought it, he moved away, going to the window and looking out at the lightning flashing in the distance.

"Did you sign anything?" he asked, not turning.

"What difference does it make?" she said flatly, her voice reflecting sudden fatigue.

Cade came swiftly across the room and grabbed her shoulders. "Did you actually put pen to paper and make the deal? Tell me!"

"Yes, yes...and it was a good deal," she insisted, half belligerently and half pleading with him to support her action. More quietly, she asked, "Why aren't you happy for me, Cade?"

"Elizabeth..." He shook his head, denying whatever sentence he had been about to speak. "Just...leave it." She placed her hand lightly on his arm, but he stiffened as if touched by something frightening or something foul. "I don't want to get involved. This isn't any good. Taking it any further at all is only going to make things worse.''

"Make what worse?" she asked, withdrawing her touch. "I don't understand why everything always has to be worse with us. Why can't things be better?"

For the first time she realized that he was actually trembling. She thought the cause was rage, but there was a look of such torment about his face that she had to revise her initial opinion.

"Because they can't.'' With a shove, he moved her aside and strode through the room into the hall and up the stairs without looking back.

She merely stood where she was, dumbfounded by his reaction. Upstairs, she heard his door close shut. A second later, she heard what sounded like a heavy object being hurled against the wall. A crack of thunder came right after, and the foundation of the house shivered beneath her feet.

Cade stared at the blood coming from the break in the skin where he had slammed his knuckles against the wall. He was not a violent man, but control was beyond him now. Everything was turning against him.

On his desk lay the opened letter, handed to him by none other than Elizabeth herself. She had no idea, of course, that the letter sealed her fate. It was a virtual death sentence for the mill. The letter had advised him that the corporation papers he had filed for what was to be his blind for doing business in Greenridge had finally cleared. The Phoenix Corporation officially lived.

To hurry the deal along he had had to disappear occasionally, meeting with financial men in Charleston and once flying to New York overnight. And tomorrow the announcement would appear, as long planned, in the Greenridge paper, telling the citizens of a new textile mill to be built in town.

And Elizabeth had just this day signed away her property—the only thing she was going to have left in the world!—to save a mill which had no chance in hell of surviving now that he was moving in for the big kill.

It was what he had planned for—her destruction. Well now he had it. Hooray.

He sank down on his bed, his head swimming in circles. *God!* What had he done? He had fallen in love with the woman. He *loved* her! It wasn't even lust or infatuation. It was love, the whole ball of wax. What should have been his own brilliant moment of satisfaction felt more like a knife wound in his gut.

Chapter Twelve

The inevitable storm broke two hours later. It came all at once with the anticipated fury. Anticlimactic, it seemed to Elizabeth, whose inner world seemed far more tumultuous as she gazed out at the rain and light slashing across the sky.

The scene with Cade had left her severely shaken. Lately she had come not to expect too much of life, but in this instance she had been so sure of having done the smart thing, she had lost all caution. She had hoped for a happy evening of celebration.

That certainly had been a mistake!

In one way she felt her life was growing, at last moving ahead. She felt good about it. There was no doubt that she had done the intelligent, even the courageous thing, by agreeing to sell the land. Otherwise the land would just go on sitting there as it had for centuries, like a vain woman lolling about watching, while the rest of the world moved out of sight. Eventually, if she didn't have the funds to support herself, the house and all the property would have to be sold anyway. By offering it for sale now, she would have cash to invest in the mill, thereby increasing her chance to keep things going.

It was sad, of course, to sell something that had been a part of her family's history for so long; it wasn't that she was immune to a sense of regret. The truth was, nostalgia flowed thick as molasses through her environment. Wherever she looked, she was reminded of easier times, happier times when the worst things that happened, happened to other people, and generally those she didn't know. Up until Edward's death her life in Greenridge was blessedly isolated from the ugliness lying beyond her own property lines.

As a girl, she and her friends would occasionally catch rumblings of unpleasantness existing on the fringes of their lives. There was something about a lynching once, archaic as it had sounded even then, and another time snatches of muted adult conversation told of a suicide.

Trouble had once even glanced off her own family's fortunes. It was all very vague, but she knew her father had met with other of the town's nabobs to discuss what to do with the cheeky leader of an insurrection against their mill. The man was attempting to unionize the mill's labor force. Eventually the situation must have exploded into some sort of confrontation. Elegant and reserved at all times, her father had returned one evening with an uncharacteristic and disorienting wildness to his personality.

As she looked out on her lawn fast becoming a lake, she recalled that night. She had been frightened of the change in her father. Seeing him in that state, she felt she hardly knew him. It was as if the family's pet had suddenly turned into a wild beast. She had at that time been enamored with colorful historical novels romanticizing life in European courts and telling tales of swashbuckling over high seas. The phrase "blood in his eye" suddenly loomed in her mind as she had stared at her father who was drinking bourbon like water and braying epithets of revenge and of justice meted.

To this very night, she never knew what the matter had been. It had been serious, of course, but when she attempted to discover its nature there seemed to be a conspiracy of silence on all levels. Certainly whatever her father knew about the incident became a forbidden topic in their relationship. Other of Elizabeth's friends met with the same refusal by their parents to discuss that day's events. Eventually the mystery had gone the way of everything else in her life, dwindling to hazy inconsequential reflections, which in turn were eventually pushed out of her consciousness altogether.

The past for her was therefore almost completely devoid of unhappy memories, and for that reason her surroundings took on the rosy mellow glow of those happier times, making her current straits all the more severe in comparison.

Surely Cade had to understand that what she had done was sensible. But he had gone berserk when she had told him. It was as if she had committed some deliberate, unpardonable act against him. Loving him was a fact of her being, but the pain such love exacted seemed at this moment too great a price to pay. There was a limit to such pain, and she asked herself if perhaps that threshold of endurance had been crossed.

A sudden wind had come up and a wave of rain drove against her. She was stepping back just as a bolt of lightning sizzled and arched directly overhead. For an instant the night burst into white fire, illuminating the terrain. In the eerie light, the normal shapes of trees and fence posts and even the wooden swing in the side yard, took on tortured, unfamiliar patterns. The world beyond her room looked gnarled and surrealistic, as if she were being shown a negative of life as seen from another dimension.

All went dark again. Then a mad concert rocked the heavens and the world exploded in silver light.

Elizabeth cringed, hands flying to her ears, eyes closing out the river of light that came whipping down again and again in frenzied slashes. A sharp crack resounded as a tree was victimized somewhere nearby.

But a more horrible sound, even more bloodcurdling than the cataclysmic overture, pierced through Elizabeth's thin wall of defense. A human wail, a woman's shrill keening cut through the atmosphere.

Elizabeth's eyes shot open. Directly below, a form stood in the drive. Stunned, Elizabeth watched the brief, flickering image of a woman alternately appear and disappear as the lightning flashed. The rain drove in a gray slant and obscured the woman's features behind a watery veil. But even so, Elizabeth made out the wide frightened eyes, and lips parted in abject terror.

There was darkness again, and by the next illumination the woman was gone.

Cade watched from his room as the storm moved in for its first great assault. There was a certain thrill to it, a kind of masculine power wielded by nature with which he could identify. Would that he could be as impersonally effective in his own imminent campaign of destruction. He did not taste any pleasure in the certainty that he would soon be a conqueror.

The world beneath him quaked from the sonorous reverberations. The air burst open, the night shattering in a series of blinding flashes. In front of all this, he remained emotionally unmoved, watching the terrible and dazzling play of nature with a sense of removal. It was necessary. He was resigned to experience life in this way, at a distance calculated to save him from feelings which could only bring on more pain. Foolishly, he had thought he could lease happiness in small doses. He thought he could trick destiny for a brief span of time during his liaison with Elizabeth. But he had been caught in his own web, and now all around he heard the gods wrathful laughter.

Lost in his gloom, he did not at first connect the searing shriek with reality. But suddenly, the night shimmered with electricity, and below him a shape came boldly into view. It was a woman. She was directly before him, her arms rising above her, hands flat as if she hoped to hold back the storm by her feeble protest of splayed fingers.

The light suddenly died, and blackness prevailed. A raging torrent of water cascaded against the roof and outside walls. When the next bolt raced across the horizon, the woman had disappeared.

Cade reacted at once. He flew from his room and down the stairs, yanking open the door and rushing into the downpour. Wild, he ran against the driving rain, turning about in search of the woman he had seen.

He raised his head and looked toward the house, saw Elizabeth standing just inside the door of her balcony.

"Stay there!" he shouted. "Lock your door. Stay there!"

But she couldn't hear him. He pushed his body against the storm and made for the house.

She was waiting for him at the top of the stairs, and when he started up, she ran down, meeting him halfway.

Her arms were thrown around him and he felt the heat of her body take the chill of his own and convert it to warmth.

"You saw her! You saw her, too! What does she want? What *can* she want?" Elizabeth cried. "I'm so afraid, Cade. Her face...God, like a ghost." Elizabeth looked at him, eyes wide as if she had perhaps just seen one. "She isn't one, is she? She was real, wasn't she?" She was speaking so fast, her tongue tripped several times.

"She's real," Cade murmured. His arms held her tightly. "Come on," he said, and turned her back to climb the stairs with him. He held her close even as they ascended, and he knew then he could not go through his vengeful enterprise unscathed, as he had hoped. Nor could he stop what had been set into motion, and in truth, what he still felt had to be done if he were to live with himself. He had always ended such a thought with the phrase, "in peace." But there was no peace to be had ever for him. He knew that now. He felt somehow disembodied, or more correctly, dis-ensouled, as he walked with Elizabeth down the hall. His fate was to circle purgatory forever, a life lived in an eternity between heaven and hell.

Elizabeth made no noises of protest when he drew her into his room and locked the door behind. It was only when he began to undress out of his wet clothes that he noticed her uncertainty.

"You're damp from leaning against me," he said, draping his shirt on the back of a chair where it could dry. "Undress and come to bed."

"But—"

He knew what she was thinking, and of course she had every right to her confused reticence. "Elizabeth," he said, then waited for a thunderous upheaval in the heavens to subside before continuing. "I love you," he said. "I love you," he said again. "For the record, you were right about everything you said earlier."

"I'm not keeping records." She looked at the bed, at him, and out to the storm. They seemed of one piece, each a symbol of dissension. "It's best that I go to my own room."

"You're afraid," he countered. "Stay."

"I'm more afraid of having to go through—"

"I know," he said, and crossed quickly to her, taking her hands in his and with his head bent, kissed her fingers. "I will always love you, Elizabeth," he said. "I have always loved you. From that first time I saw you." He closed his eyes, knowing that what they were thinking in their minds would be different, and hating himself for not—even in this moment of baring his soul—being able to speak the whole truth as it was. His love was from their youth, and it had raged through the fantasies of his adult life, until he returned to Greenridge to murder those impossible dreams once and for all.

"I can't anymore, Cade . . . somehow it's got to end. This craziness of love in the moonlight and in the daylight the—"

"No, no..." he said, and kissed her with such force that her lips felt bruised when he drew away. "Tonight you must stay with me. You must."

"And in the morning? It will be like the others," she answered for him.

"Do you believe I love you?" he asked, agonized.

"Yes. I know you do. But there's so much else that I don't know, that for some reason you won't tell me."

"Oh, Elizabeth." He drew her back to him. His skin was hot and still damp from the storm. "Have you ever felt that in spite of all you do, all the plans, and the efforts expended so diligently in the name of some goal, we are nothing more than pawns? We are being moved about and allowed to think we are autonomous."

"When Edward died," she said, "it seemed so. But that has nothing to do with us."

"Perhaps it has everything to do with us." Cade sighed. "What if you were dealt a hand that was unplayable, but you were made to stay in the game?"

"I'd leave the game."

"No, you couldn't. That's the very point. You couldn't walk away. That stupid, cruel hitch was as much a part of the game as the hand you were dealt, you see. You were given cards that had to be played out, but you knew they had no real value, and yet you were not able to leave the game."

"Maybe there was something else besides winning the game you were supposed to learn," she said.

Suddenly, Cade's expression changed. He appeared alert, almost energized. "What?"

"What?" she repeated.

"You just said something...that there was something to learn...that maybe the cards weren't the issue... Maybe," he said, drifting into an internal region as he followed the thread of thought, "the issue is to discover the issue." He came out of himself and looked directly into her eyes. There was pleading there. There was a vulnerability he had never before shown. "Stay," he said again. "Let's see what the morning will bring."

The storm raged on. They lay in bed, wrapped together, listening as the wind grew into something more serious than the initial strong gusts. Beyond the shutters fastened against the storm, the gale howled like a demonic banshee.

The passion, usually so quick to kindle between them, came more slowly and with a connection that was as emotional as it was physical.

"I love you," Cade said twice, each time holding her face between his hands, searching her eyes for acknowledgment that his message was received and accepted.

A fullness came over her, joy and sadness, a euphoric sense of completeness. Her fingers traced the sharp outline of his high cheekbones, swept away a lock of dark hair from his forehead, moved lightly over his lips. And the sweet fullness grew in her heart, expanding, overwhelming in its intensity. The mere words "I love you" that she would have returned at any other time, were now small lost particles against the vast beauty of her experience. He was so much more to her than the three words. He was everything, life itself!

"Cade," she whispered, and in that single word, the entire world seemed to swirl in her heart.

The morning seemed never to come. But finally, it was not the light seeping through the shutters, but the silence that woke Elizabeth. She was as surprised to find that she had drifted off to sleep as she was to find the world calm again. Occasionally, a trickle of water would course down from some tree or a rain gutter. Other than that, there was an exquisite kind of peace.

It was also how she felt. At peace.

Beside her, Cade still slept. He looked beautiful, the thick row of lashes curled against the tanned skin. His beard was dark, its stubble bearing out the rough force of his male nature. How unlike Edward he was, how different from Mason Philips. With Cade as a comparison, they seemed petty and colorless, their sexuality wrapped up in inconsequential social trivia.

For a while she watched his breathing and, thinking better of waking him, decided to dress and take stock of the outside world. She dreaded the damage that had likely occurred.

Slipping into one of Cade's shirts, she crossed the room and opened the shutters for her first glance at the destruction. Surprisingly, the world seemed to sparkle. Trailing wisps of darkness, like straggling demons sulkily departing, were all that remained of the night's vengeance. The sun appeared high above, a magnificent benevolent presence.

Elizabeth's eyes fell to the earth where tree branches lay severed from trunks and dislodged shingles from the roof floated serenely on the surface of a small newly formed lake on her front property. It was a mess. But that was all right, she thought, the indomitable sense of joy still with her.

Now she had everything. She had herself and Cade's love. Whatever else came or went, merely came or went. The center of her world, that incomparable feeling of love, would never alter.

With that certainty, she turned and gathered up her nightgown from the side of the bed, and was thinking of what she would make for their breakfast, when her eyes fell upon the papers unfurled across Cade's desk.

It was not snooping. It was merely that the papers were there in clear view and she was right beside them. She might even have moved on, but for the large block printing across the top which caught her attention.

Phoenix Textile Mill, Greenridge South Carolina.

At first she thought it had to be a weird optical illusion, some trick her mind was playing on her. But of course it wasn't.

She felt as if everything in her was fast draining from her body—all strength, all sense of reality, all hope, all love. She felt for the edge of the desk and sank into the chair before it. It was hard to breathe, at first because she had forgotten to, and then because the shock made it almost impossible. Her mind had splintered into a thousand pieces, shards of it flying into space, making it impossible to concentrate on what was before her.

Horrified, she wanted to run from the sight; yet a strange wisdom rose up from within and compelled her to suffer what had to be endured.

Her eyes raced over the blue-and-white schematic, identifying it as not only the layout for an automated textile mill, but also as one of the rolls of paper Cade had carried back and forth with him on those occasions when he had disappeared for a day or two. But of course. He had gone to the city. He had met with the engineering and architectural firm listed on the prints. He had been working on his plans from the beginning.

With shaking fingers, she reached to the corner of the desk and drew an envelope with the letter beneath it, closer. It was the special delivery letter that had come yesterday for him. A glance and the final spike was driven into her heart. It was the notification from a New

York bank for full funding of his mill operation to be established in Greenridge, South Carolina. They wished him a profitable venture, and a long and friendly association with their lending institution.

She wished him hell.

Another sheaf of papers caught her eye. These were neat, columnar spread sheets filled with numbers. Her fingers swept down the lists at the projections, and the plan he was implementing became as clear in her mind as it had to be in his. He was going to ruin her.

For a moment, stunned, she could only sit there. Cade stirred slightly, as if influenced by the intensity of her thoughts. No woman ever wronged by a man could have felt such anger as she did that moment. Her breathing switched from ragged and shallow, to a deeper, more controlled pattern.

The fury she had felt a moment before also changed. It did not abate. Instead it was transmuted from wild, directionless energy to form a cold purposeful resolution to survive.

Other than Cade and herself, there was no one else in the house that morning as Elizabeth put a pot of coffee on in the kitchen. Those boarders who had been absent earlier in the evening, had obviously been unable to return later. The house was like a tomb.

She unfastened the shutters, one by one, moving as a sleepwalker through the rooms and corridors of the old mansion. She imagined the ghostly figures of her ancestors following beside her, their heads gravely bent in companionable recognition of her misery.

But as still as the house was, she was even more quiet within. There was a deadliness to her center now, as if the eye of a storm resided there.

Sometime later—perhaps an hour had passed, time to Elizabeth now seemed inconsequential—she heard Cade's footsteps start down the stairs.

"Elizabeth?" he called.

His voice was a warm breeze in the house. Elizabeth looked from where she sat at the table, to the window. Beyond, the wet leaves of trees glistened like a million emeralds. The world was adorned in myriad splendor. Inside, she was cold and gray. She waited.

"Elizabeth!" Cade said. He stood in the dining room door, smiling across to her. Smiling at her!

She glanced up, looking over the top of her coffee cup which she raised to her lips. He had put on jeans and a simple black sweatshirt, sleeves cut off short and frayed at the edges. How handsome he was—broad shoulders, small tapering waist, compact buttocks, thighs muscular and tight. His body was magnificent. She would never forget its feel, not in a thousand lifetimes. His smile was perfection itself, teeth even and bright, the lips softly curled at the corners. Oh, and the eyes! Those amazing, extraordinary green lanterns outshone any light and compelled her to forget her pride, to forget her very wits when he cast their hypnotic force upon her.

"Good morning," she said pleasantly.

Perhaps he sensed something in her extreme calm, for she noted that he did a slight take when she spoke, as if the words did not measure up to some prescribed level.

"Good morning," he answered back, and negotiating the distance between them, bent and kissed her neck in two places.

She merely smiled. "Coffee?"

"Yeah, great," he said, and when she started to rise to get it from the sideboard, he urged her down with a slight touch of his hand.

Behind her, she heard the liquid fill his cup. "I must have been out like a light," he said, coming back around and taking a seat.

"You were," she said.

This time he did not immediately jump back in with a comment. Instead he observed her silently. She stared back.

"So," he said. "You saw them."

Elizabeth did not look away. "Yes."

Cade nodded. He bit the inside of his lip, then looked to the window. "The legal term is 'conflict of interest.'"

"Our relationship wasn't a contractual agreement."

"No," he said. "It wasn't." He exhaled long and slowly.

"Tell me," Elizabeth said, "I'm curious. Did you want me to find the papers this morning? Is that why they were there for me, all spread out so neatly along with the letter from the bank? I mean it certainly did save you from having to make a long speech. Clever of you. You were able to avoid a messy scene. Sleeping so soundly, too, while I—"

"No. I didn't even think of the papers being there. I'd completely forgotten them."

"Oh. Well, we all goof up sometimes. Don't let it get you down," she said. "More coffee?"

He ignored her, of course. Beneath the placid exterior, her insides churned. But she was determined to end her part of the fiasco with some semblance of dignity. His eyes were on her, and in an instant's realization, she knew somehow that he had been waiting all along for this moment of confrontation. In fact, the impression that their entire relationship had in some way been carefully orchestrated and arranged and guided to this one particular point in time, was so compelling, that Elizabeth had to ask, "Was it worth all the buildup? Getting to this moment?"

He looked shocked. "I don't know what you mean." The words had the sound of dry leaves rattling across hard earth.

"Never mind," Elizabeth said. "Of course I want you out of here this morning," she said evenly. "You and everything you own."

Cade sank back against his chair and nodded. His thoughts flew inward, the green crystalline gaze turning cloudy.

"Why?" she whispered. "What had I ever done to you? Wouldn't ruining a business have been enough for you. Did you have to kill me, too? Did you have to take my soul and tear holes through it—holes that can never, not ever be mended? Why," Elizabeth asked, "why did you use me like that?"

Cade pushed himself from the table. He took several steps to the door, then turned partially around, just enough that their eyes could join a final time. "I loved you," he said. "It was because I loved you and could never have you."

"So you had to murder me?"

"Yes," he said. "It was like that."

He walked from the room without looking back.

A few minutes later Elizabeth heard his footsteps coming down the stairs and the slam of the front door soon after. She watched him from the dining room window as he drove away. No tears came. She had always expected that there would be tears when the end finally came. But there wasn't anyone left to cry.

She had been slain by Cade as surely and finally as Roy Buck had murdered Edward on that beautiful summer's day. Only Edward was more fortunate. He had gone away body and soul, maybe to someplace better. Maybe to no place at all. But at least he didn't have to keep going, a body without a being attached to it.

Elizabeth pulled herself up from the chair and dragged herself to the window. *Cade, I loved you so. Cade, my darling, my darling . . . I wish you all the hell I now feel. If there is justice, God . . . let it be so.*

Chapter Thirteen

It was the end of October and along with so much else in Greenridge the long, seemingly eternal summer had come to a close.

Elizabeth steered the car down the wide drive leading to the noble estate her ancestors had built and inhabited for so many generations—what was left of the noble estate, that was. The bulk of it had been sectioned off, and already bulldozers were industriously breaking ground at the edges of the property. True to the developer's reputation, he got in fast and by the looks of it, would be getting out fast. Good, she thought. Maybe the whole enterprise would be less painful that way. She could stand a little relief from prolonged misery.

She had been at the mill all day, and the time spent poring over figures and fielding the irate calls of vendors wanting payment for merchandise shipped ages ago, was exhausting.

In the twilight, she saw how a few leaves had already turned color. Soon enough the oaks would be bare. Mornings, lately, were cooler. Idly, she thought of taking out the warmer blankets. It would conserve on heat. Winter's expenses were just another thing to dread.

This season had certainly racked up its share of casualties. Elizabeth included her life as one of them. Oh, she had gotten on—and she still did, one foot after the next, one breath out, one breath in—yet she counted herself as nothing more than an automaton. She kept her mind on the mechanical aspects of living. It was the most she could handle. If, God help her, she allowed the slightest emotion to creep past her icy shield, there would be no telling what could happen.

Sometimes she would lie awake at night, thinking she could turn out to be one of those crazy people who get talked about on news shows after they climb a tower and start firing on a crowd of innocent people. "She was always such a lovely person. So quiet. Refined. It's impossible that she could do something so terrible. She must have just snapped." Yes, that was it exactly. The emotions were there, somewhere beneath the surface, and building. She might deny their existence, but they were there lurking about just the same. Busy, that was the ticket. She had better not stop her treadmill activity or she might be off climbing towers one day.

After the storm the weather had remained hot, but intermittently there had been rain—gentle, not torrential—to relieve the earth and the spirits of those who lived above it. Nothing however appeared to come close to resembling that terrible supernatural tempest of her last night with Cade Delaney. Nor did she ever, after that time, catch sight of the woman who had stood below her window like a dispossessed wraith.

As for Cade—she steeled herself at the thought of him, knowing how important it was to maintain a perspective of emotional distance—she had not crossed his path since the day he had left her house. She knew that he was still in town, for there was talk at the mill and in general when she accompanied Mason to the Country Club, that Cade was continuing on with his project. During these conversations, she had trained her mind to go off on faraway trips, and no one suspected that the nods and smiles weren't connected to the social discourse being conducted.

There was one additional incident concerning the woman, however, that drove her close to calling the police. In the end she decided against it, partially because she knew the police wouldn't be able to figure anything out and also because any reminder of the woman was a reminder of Cade. In her present state, any thought of Cade was more threatening to her welfare than the physical menace posed by the woman. Anyway, as Elizabeth saw herself, she was for all intents and purposes no more than an empty shell of a human being existing on borrowed time and borrowed money. She had nothing major to lose by pressing her luck when it came to physical safety.

She had come home late one night after being at the mill. At the time there were only two boarders in residence—a woman who was hard of hearing and a man who seemed to have a girlfriend on the edge of town and invariably stayed out late at night. Neither of them could have told her anything about what had transpired in her absence.

On the night in question, she had been wearily picking her way up the steps to the front veranda when her shoe sent something flying. Upon inspection, she found it to be a gold circular pin, nothing of any value. Her first thought was that it belonged to her female boarder. She put it in her pocket to give to her later. But then she noted the porch chair turned over on its side, and beside the chair and several feet away, scuff marks, as if a battle had ensued.

Her blood had turned a bit colder as her mind took a fast trip through a series of old headlines screaming mayhem, and in spite of her lack of enthusiasm for life, she was hesitant to enter the house. But just then she heard the woman boarder humming to herself up above, and her fears dissolved.

There was no explanation forthcoming about the pin. The female boarder denied it was hers, just as she denied hearing any commotion on the porch.

That incident had taken place two weeks previous. Since then, there had been no further sign of trouble. Perhaps at some other time she might have pursued the mystery to its denouement, but she did not currently have the emotional capacity to involve herself in anything more than the mill's operation. She was tougher now, but not so tough that she would go seeking trouble to add to her already precarious position in life.

Changes were not just in the weather, but in her. For one thing, she was certainly no longer merely a pretty Southern belle. Gone was the perennial debutante she had been before Edward's death. Her appearance was even different. It was less studied, emphasizing character rather than fashion. Her manner had become efficient and at times, some said, brusque. Recently she had become aware that some people did not like her new ways. The world she had once thought she owned did not like a woman who talked back to it.

Mason, for instance, was definitely unhappy with her. When he discovered she had sold her property to continue the operation of the mill, one might have thought she had stolen it from him. He berated her over martinis at the Club.

"Elizabeth, I'm stunned."

"It was a smart thing to do, Mason. The only thing to do."

"No. You could have married me. Instead you did this . . . this amazing thing. Why it's almost unthinkable that you could have done something like this . . . you, Elizabeth, of all people."

"I need to eat too, Mason. Just like all people."

"Fine, but you were meant to eat steak, not hamburger. You were meant to live in an estate, not with some suburban slum lapping over your property lines. My Lord," Mason said, looking revolted, "it's unthinkable."

Anyway, her smart move had managed to keep her barely, just ever so marginally solvent. But after she had paid the overdue principal on the loans and the staggeringly exorbitant late charges, she had little left to effect creative solutions to make the mill profitable.

On the last evening of October, she found herself as weary as she had ever been as she all but shuffled up the stairs of the veranda, into the hall, and through the kitchen, looking for something easy and quick to eat before calling it a day.

It was pathetic. She stood before the opened refrigerator, her eyes searching from row to row, scanning the contents as if a book. There were more or less blank pages—a few celery sticks, a dying tomato, something orange and indistinguishable, various condiments with nothing to accompany them. Pathetic, pathetic. How the mighty have fallen. In the end, a bowl of split pea soup sustained her. She made a note to buy some food before she dropped dead.

Upstairs, she bathed and climbed into bed with the newspaper. It was the latest issue of the Greenridge Bulletin and had come out as it always did on Thursday. It got printed once a week, news or no news. Any way you cut it, there was only gossip to be reported anyway. Elizabeth leafed quickly through the first page, which showed some smiling faces of her friends—former friends—who had sold more lace doilies at a church function than any other time in the history of Greenridge and had contributed the sum of four hundred and fifty dollars to a local chapter of the 4H Club, where their sons were leaders. A pure example of recycled wealth. Other such monumental stories appeared in due succession, and Elizabeth was on her way to being bored to sleep when she caught sight of a rather startling block of print.

First of all it was startling for the fact that it was a real advertisement. It looked as though it had been done professionally in some major metropolis by some slick advertising firm. And secondly, it was worth a second glance because it was running on the third page of the paper, which was usually dedicated to gardening awards and advice about nematodes. But there it sat, smack dab on page three, taking up valuable space that could have been devoted to tomato blight. Elizabeth smiled with satisfaction that some ancient rule of Greenridge order had been desecrated by putting a genuine commercial advertisement in a different place.

And then the smile faded.

There in large black letters was her death warrant, signed, sealed, and delivered.

The Phoenix Mill was hiring personnel. The wages listed were higher than those offered by her mill, and higher than those she could meet even if she had to sell her blood. Most of the people she and Edward had let go had long since moved from the town, unable to find employment. The only people available now were those she employed to keep the barest level of production still going. If Cade took them, she was finished. And of course, he would take them.

Mason locked the door to his office and made certain his drapes were pulled closed. His secretary was still outside at her desk typing up some last-minute letters, and he didn't want to be discovered having a small nip. He kept the flask of bourbon in the back of his side drawer, carefully concealed. There was also a lock to discourage intrusion. In this place, he kept his little secrets about the people of his town, tidy dossiers that could make him stronger and break those whose time had come to be broken. The drawer was like his diary. It was also like his confessor, for every trespass he committed was also duly recorded in the files of those he acted against. In this way he felt somewhat cleansed of the deed. Stored in his file, he did not need to clutter up his conscience with guilt.

In a few minutes he could sign the letters and go off to the Greenridge Inn where he would have a drink, catch up on some local gossip, perhaps have dinner, and later call Elizabeth to soft-soap her a bit more. He settled down into his large executive chair, took a swig from the flask, and while enjoying the taste, opened the latest copy of the Bulletin, just delivered.

The first page, the second, a sweeping glance down the third which was devoted to gardening and therefore had no social value to him, and then—

He stared at the newsprint before him. He looked at it so hard and for so long that it began to waver before his eyes. His eyes burned from dryness brought on by the intense concentration, and a slight upsurge of nausea overtook him. He took a series of quick, deep swallows of the liquor.

The liquor burned. He should not drink. His doctor told him that again and again. Besides, it hurt like hell sometimes. But that was all right. He rather enjoyed the pain, thinking it was making him tough, preparing him for some future test of fortitude. He was always thinking of the future. Forward movement was always the antidote to the quivering fear that arose whenever he felt he was falling behind in the parade. This fear, that others were gaining on him and that he would eventually be left behind, trampled and forgotten as a heap on the side of the road, had plagued him his entire life. As his enemy the fear crippled; as his ally he turned fear's power to his advantage and used its energy to spur him on to destroy whatever obstacle or foe appeared in his path.

His mind raced ahead. It leapt out of control, not just leading the parade but straying off the route in a desperate attempt to find some way to put order back into the neat world he had constructed for himself. Mason knew he had to calm himself. Nothing but more confusion would come out of this panic. Gradually, he forced his mind down from its manic heights and began to consider the situation logically from its various angles.

Cade Delaney was the Phoenix Corporation. The Phoenix Corporation was going into direct competition with Elizabeth's mill.

Mason reflected further. If Elizabeth did not marry him, then he could not get his hands on the equipment and inventory that would be sold at auction to pay off the loans owed the bank. Everything would be lost to him. Certainly he could always buy the mill later, but it would need new equipment. That would be far too expensive anyway, and now totally out of the question with a competitor in the same geographical location.

Therefore his course was clear and narrow. He would have to marry Elizabeth posthaste; and he would have to destroy Cade Delaney as quickly. Mason took another drink from the flask and, gripping the edge of the desk, suffered its effects bravely.

It was nine o'clock when Cade entered the Greenridge Inn. He had been at the mill all day, watching over the electrical installation of some of the high-powered mill equipment that would soon be turning out both natural and synthetic fibers.

"Evening, Mr. Delaney," said the desk clerk when he arrived.

The man looked at him queerly, then flicked his eyes briefly to the side as if conferring with an outside source as to what he was to say next.

Cade also looked. He understood at once. Through the wide opening of the lobby, he could see into the cocktail lounge where Mason and several of his cronies were seated at a round table. Their eyes were on him.

Cade met their stares for a moment, just long enough to convey that he was not afraid, then turned back to the clerk whose demeanor seemed that of an ambulance chaser, apprehension tinged with exhilaration.

"My key, please," Cade ordered evenly.

"Uh, they, the gentlemen in there, would like you to join them."

"The key," Cade said again.

"But—"

Cade moved around to the side of the desk and retrieved his own key from the slot. Then he walked into the room where the five men were seated stiff as dried mortar, watching him. They looked like gun slingers who had called a shootout with a fastgun they had never seen before, and were now having second thoughts about the contest.

All but Mason, that is.

Mason, dressed impeccably in a three-piece beige suit and light blue dress shirt with a smart yellow and blue tie, perfect for the in-between season, eyed him with a look of cold amusement. It was the look of a man playing poker with an ace up his sleeve. Cade was not afraid of Philips, but he was not fool enough to underestimate him either.

"Good evening," Mason said in an exaggerated drawl. "I believe that congratulations are in order."

An open copy of the newspaper was visible on the table. It was turned to the gardening section.

"I'm tired, Philips. What is it you want?"

"I want us to talk."

"About what? We've got nothing to say to each other. I'm an independent agent in this town. No ties to your bank. No ties to your social network. No ties, period."

Mason's features hardened, the lids of his eyes dropping slightly as if the action went along with some internal shifting of gears. Slowly, he rose up from his seat with an assurance that came from a man who was accustomed to getting his own way. He hitched his head slightly to Cade, and said, "Mr. Delaney, it is in your best interests to speak with me."

Cade went along, primarily out of curiosity. In his fantasies of revenge, nurtured over the years, he would have savored an opportunity like this. But now he didn't. He was truly tired, physically and spiritually. He was just running out the plan which had to be run out because years ago destiny had set the events into motion, and his part was to be the driver of the vehicle of destruction. God, he was tired of it all.

Mason commandeered a corner table in the lounge and ordered himself a drink, asking Cade what he would like.

"To get to the point," Cade said.

"Bring Mr. Delaney a Scotch and water. That's a good slick drink for a good slick Yankee like yourself, isn't it?"

Cade waited.

"Okay, I'll put it to you simply. Delaney, this is my town, more or less. In case you haven't noticed."

Cade nodded slightly, acknowledging that he was listening but not necessarily agreeing.

"I keep a balance between being above the crowd and being a good friend to all, even those on the downside of their luck. So I have no real enemies. Or another way to put it is I've got a lot of friends here. And they'd go out of their way to help me if I let it be known that I needed it." Mason paused. "I can see that I may need to ask my friends to do me some favors."

Again Cade said nothing. He merely waited.

Mason leaned forward. "You are not wanted in my town. You cause me trouble. You are interfering with plans I have set up and have worked long and hard for over the years. Now I am telling you clear, Mr. Delaney, to get out of here on your own. This town does not need your mill. And I don't need you here to muck things up."

Cade waited a moment. Then he rose. "Good," he said. "I'm glad you're so popular. And I thank you for laying your cards on the table. But sorry, I'm not going to do the same for you. I'd hate to spoil your surprises. I've got my own agenda, Philips. They include your destruction." Cade backed away. "Think about it," he said. "Think about if you really want to get into the ring with me."

Upstairs he threw off his clothes and took a scalding shower. Then he opened his own newspaper to the advertisement. His gut twisted as he thought of what seeing it had done to Elizabeth.

Where was the exhilaration of victory he had waited for all those many years?

It was a Pyrrhic victory; the casualties had been too costly. He had been cheated out of his love, just as surely as those men had cheated his father out of his life.

Again, as he had so many times before, he almost reacted to the impulse of bursting in on Elizabeth and coming clean about the whole affair from start to finish. He wondered how she would take the news of his true identity. In spite of his love for her—he had always loved her and always would; that at least was one constant—there had never been any doubt that they were separated by class and blood. A roll in the hay and a midsummer's infatuation, brought on by loneliness and a brooding heat that boiled one's blood and brains, was no guarantee of undying devotion if push really came to shove.

Although she had certainly changed greatly, it was likely that by marrying well she would return to being the illusive, supercilious American princess of yore. In that case, to bare his soul to her would serve no purpose, and in fact would make all his efforts, not to mention the pain he'd already suffered, nothing but one great colossal waste.

On the other hand, why would it be totally inconceivable that she had changed permanently for the good? He had. Once, he had been no more than an inconspicuous entity in Greenridge, the son of a poor man whose only social credentials were his guts to fight the status quo—and his guts got stomped on pretty hard. But he, the son of the poor man, left town for the big city, got himself a fine education, bought himself a lot of fancy duds and a ritzy condominium in a first-class neighborhood and established his own consulting firm where he dazzled folk from one coast to the other with his clever advice. The kid who had left town on a train one miserable day was a new person. Could Elizabeth Hart also make that claim?

He decided to give it a shot and find out.

An hour later, he stood before the front door and waited for her to answer his knock.

It took a long while. He heard her footsteps coming cautiously across the foyer and imagined her curiosity as to who could be beating down her door at half past ten at night. The door opened a crack.

"Elizabeth?"

The door closed.

But he did not hear footsteps fading away. So she was shocked and she hated him no doubt—definitely, she hated him—but she was still standing on the opposite side of the door. Meaning there was hope.

"Look, I know how much you must be hating me now. I totally sympathize with your feelings. But there's more to the story than you can guess and—"

The door opened wide. Elizabeth stood on the opposite side of the screen, the gray mesh giving her a misty appearance. She was bundled in a heavy green terry robe and her hair was partially up, the rest of it hanging down in strands. Cade realized she must have recently come from the shower. He longed to grab her in his arms and sweep her up the stairs into her bedroom, into her bed, remove the robe and make love to her the entire night.

That was only a mad fantasy, however. The woman staring at him would just as soon cut out his heart as shake his hand.

"Get off my property," she said steadily. The coldness was that of solid ice.

"I want to explain—"

"Oh, please," she said. "The paper explained quite nicely."

"The mill has nothing to do with you and me. That's what I want to tell you."

"Nothing to do...?" She shook her head and laughed. "You have taken my entire life today. Because of you I have forfeited my property. Because of you I have lost my chance at earning a decent livelihood. Because of trusting you, I have proven myself a stupid, naive, addle-headed woman. Isn't that enough? What the hell more do you have to take from me? There's nothing left, damn you. Except maybe, just possibly a small amount of self-respect for having the good sense to tell you to clear off my property and out of my life."

"It's not that way—"

"You have just run out of charm," she said, and the door closed in his face.

He considered knocking again, but knew it wouldn't do any good. The damage had been done. Fleetingly he thought of returning to the hotel and writing a long letter, baring his soul, proclaiming his love, begging for mercy, the whole works. But she had certainly made her points clear. And she was right. No matter what his motivation—whether confused or misguided or the actions of an obsessed, deranged man—the results to her life remained the same.

Before he got into his car, he looked up to her window. He thought she might be watching him; if so, it would be a sign that all was not lost. But there was no such fortunate omen. The light to her bedroom was on and clearly there was no one who cared enough to catch a fleeting glimpse of his departure. The window was quite devoid of life.

Elizabeth sat at her desk, listening to the sound of Cade's car drive off. Who drove that vehicle, she wondered? Was it the man she had loved, and whom she had truly believed had loved her? Or was it the cold-blooded bastard who had used her, played her like a fool, and finally saw that she was destroyed.

What could he possibly have said to her that could have changed anything? Nothing. And if she had let him in, no doubt, she would just have believed another of his lies. His charm had not really run out. But her willingness to accept abuse certainly had. She had to survive somehow, and that meant never, never letting him into her life again.

Chapter Fourteen

The following day Elizabeth allowed Mason the opportunity to fawn over her during lunch. He was really a jerk, she thought, as he gushed on and on about the ridiculous social rites being enacted by the town's elite. There was this party and that, and there was going to be a bus to take them to see the opera in Charleston, dinner beforehand at some French place, very posh, and on and on, until Elizabeth thought she might fall asleep in her chocolate mousse.

Nevertheless, her instincts, finely tuned over the past several months by having to read beyond false smiles, warned her that there was some purpose to this meeting which she would do well to respect.

The Club's dining room seemed filled with the town's high and mighty that day. If Mason had wanted to trot out all the trappings of her formerly cushy life to compare with her current drab existence, he could not have selected a more appropriate time or setting. Everything was pretty. As it was finally fall, there were adorable little horns of plenty as centerpieces on each table, which had ingeniously been filled with rust and gold chrysanthemums. The tablecloths themselves were of a buttery hue. A fire with real logs crackled in the large hearth, more for appearance than for warmth. Outside the large windows, the trees were sporting the barest hint of color. Ah, how cosy the world seemed from the vantage of the dining room of the Greenridge Country Club.

Women once considered friends, smiled graciously to her from other tables, and many even stopped and chatted as if it were the most natural thing in the world to include Elizabeth in the latest gossip. Of course, she was with Mason.

Elizabeth saw no reason to offend, and merely smiled and laughed and nodded her head on cue, and said that she would love to have lunch or dinner or come by for cards. Everyone would be ringing her soon. They all filtered away, no doubt feeling very pleased at their kindness and having a topic of conversation to fuel their luncheons and telephone conversations for the next few days.

Elizabeth, herself, was dressed as well as any of them. After all, hadn't she been the leader of the pack, not so long ago? She had on an expensively tailored red suit in a light wool milled by her own factory. Her purse was black snakeskin, and matched her shoes from Paris. Who would dream that beneath the vision of soft loveliness, lay a soul recently converted to stone?

No one would, Elizabeth assured herself with satisfaction and smiled winsomely at Mason who had just told her for the umpteenth time how beautiful she appeared.

Mason himself wore a boyish smile of enthusiasm when he presented to her, without forewarning, the small blue velveteen box. It was a ring box. And in it, Elizabeth found as she fought to maintain a calm exterior, was a large, rather beautiful diamond engagement ring.

"Why, Mason," she said.

"Say yes, Elizabeth?"

She found it impossible to raise her eyes. If she were to look at him now, she might either spit at him or burst into a fit of laughter. The whole thing was so absurd. How could she spend her life with a man who resembled, more than anything else to her, a piece of dry, tasteless, stale toast? They would make love—no correction...have sex; they would never, never make love—and the force of her passionate nature, awakened by Cade, would simply explode Mason into millions of little crumbs.

In spite of herself, she began to giggle, the image of Mason Philips as an exploded piece of stale toast was too ridiculous to resist. She tried to stop the sound, but in trying to check it, she only laughed harder. Soon tears were dropping down her cheeks and she was almost choking.

Through it all, Mason sat motionless. The lack of movement only served to bring greater gales of laughter from her, and from the corner of her eye she was aware now of other people staring and talking. Then she saw Mason finally move and his hand brought forth a large white envelope which he dropped in front of her.

"What's...what's..." She tried to speak, but couldn't.

"Open it, Elizabeth, and you shall find out—if you can pull yourself together long enough to do so."

The coldness in his voice was a leveling factor, and suddenly the world which had been merely a blur rose up in sharp impression. Mason's eyes bore the cold, hard appearance of gray steel. All the humor was suddenly dissipated in the knowledge that she had gone far too far this time in her cavalier attitude toward him. At heart, she knew that Mason was not a very nice man; something she had grown to sense over the past few months, regardless of his courtly charm and unctuous solicitousness. She knew it would not be a wise move to go against him.

Her fingers fumbled, as if they had an intelligence of their own and didn't want to go through with the mission of withdrawing the contents of the envelope.

"What am I going to find in here, Mason?" Elizabeth asked again.

"A little engagement present, Elizabeth."

He waited, and eventually she drew out the papers. It took only a glance to understand the legal terminology.

All feeling drained from her fingers as she dropped the pages on the table.

"So," Mason took up, his voice as cold as Death's, "I warned you. It was bound to happen sooner or later, Elizabeth. Your time has run out."

"And this is my ultimatum," she said, glancing at the ring on one side of her chocolate mousse and to the foreclosure papers on the other. "Either I marry you or I lose the mill."

"Yes. That's the way it is."

"Doesn't it bother you, Mason, that I do not love you? Not in the very least," she said, her eyes rising to his with open disdain.

"No. It doesn't bother me in the slightest. Love has nothing to do with this."

Elizabeth sank back into her chair. "Power does."

"You've become a clever woman, haven't you? Now let's see if you are smart enough to put that ring on your finger and do me the great honor of becoming my consort. Go on, impress me, Elizabeth. Dazzle me with how smart you've become."

"I like that," she said. "Your consort." She smiled. "Oh, Mason, you look like such a pale little rodent. Who would ever dream you would harbor such grand notions of conquest?"

"No one. Which is precisely why I can make my grand notions into hard realities. And, Elizabeth," he said, "don't ever call me a pale little rodent again. You may find that such creatures have very sharp teeth."

"Very well, Mason. I will consider your overwhelmingly attractive offer of marriage."

"Let me know tomorrow."

"Tomorrow?"

"I'm not waiting any longer. Oh," he said, looking around casually, "I'd like it very much if you were to smile now, Elizabeth. A lot of people have been watching this little display of yours, and I'm sure they can guess that I have just presented you with an engagement ring. Show some affection and enthusiasm."

"Mason," said Elizabeth, "I may marry you, or I may not. But one thing I refuse to do is to show an inordinate amount of enthusiasm for our alliance. Who would ever believe it? And for the time being, you need me as much as I need you. So keep your miserable threats to yourself." She moved to her feet and, turning, said over her shoulder, "Drive me home."

The next day was one that Elizabeth would never forget as long as she lived.

She awoke out of a nightmare, and for the briefest of moments experienced the relief of knowing she had only been a temporal victim of a dream world; then she remembered. What awaited her in the waking state was far more terrible than any dream. Today she would have to agree to Mason's ultimatum of marriage or suffer utter and complete financial doom.

To do so was not to prostitute her high ideals in return for gold. She simply had no high ideals left. Everything she had once valued had been stripped from her belief system. Her shining high-mindedness had dissolved into the miasmic reality of a world she had not known existed before Edward's death.

First there had been the financial disillusionment over Edward's running of the mill. Even her marriage had been false. With nothing to compare it to, she had never suspected how barren her emotional life with Edward had really been. It consisted of no more than a series of mannered social interactions. Life with Edward had been a dinner prepared without seasoning and she had survived on its blandness for years, never dreaming, never even imagining that there could be more.

Until Cade. Cade, damn him, had changed all of that. He had educated her palate to the many spices available in a relationship. For a while with Cade, life had been an exotic and tantalizing feast, and then like an itinerant peddler, he had packed up his wondrous products and left.

Women whom she had counted as her friends, had dropped her like a soiled lace handkerchief. What she had so suddenly become was too much a reminder of their own tenuous place in a shifting, unsolid world. They did not want to think too long upon the truth: that the pretty pastel rugs on which they stood could be ripped out from under them. They did not want to look at the bare truth that lay beneath those heavily padded carpets. The truth, which she had learned over the past several months in her crash course on life, was that there was nothing to support you but your own two legs. And oddly, touching that bedrock reality made life amazingly easier to manage. It did not necessarily become more pleasant, but at least existence took on an efficiency uncluttered by wishfulness. What decisions she made would now be based upon expediency and not upon the wild and inconstant ramblings of the heart. She owed Cade Delaney credit for that area of her education.

With the determination to be reasonable and to make sound decisions based upon her own best interests, she threw her blankets aside and greeted the early-morning chill, knowing that by day's end, one way or the other, her whole life will have been irrevocably altered.

She was in the mill's office—once Edward's, now her own—when the plant manager came in.

"Okay, that's it," he said. His jaw was set in a hard line and his eyes had taken on a flinty look.

"What?" Elizabeth said, already having a good suspicion.

"We've lost them. Half the work crew didn't show up this morning."

"I see. And I guess it doesn't take a crystal ball to guess why?"

"I guess not. Listen, I've gone all the way down the line with you on this, but it's plain stupid at this point to keep the doors open here. You can't run a mill without people. And you don't have the people anymore."

"I know," she said. "You're right. Well, we've given it our best shot, haven't we? There's that, at least."

"I'm sorry. I'm through here, too. I can go across the way and get myself something at Delaney's operation. I've got a wife and kids to feed. And since these doors are going to close—"

"No. Don't do that," Elizabeth said. "Not yet. The doors aren't going to close."

He stared at her, waiting for her to elaborate. "I'm going to make a deal," she said.

"I don't see as you have any bargaining power."

Elizabeth smiled ruefully. "Oh, I do...I still have something to offer." *Myself*, she thought, and not necessarily in literal terms. "One more day?"

"Just one. Then I'm gone."

When she was alone, she did not dare hesitate, for fear that she would lose her nerve and give in to whatever sentimentality and passion for Cade still lived within her. She simply had to do what she was going to do. So she dialed.

She was put through to Mason. "Elizabeth?"

"Shall we get together tonight?"

"Do we have any reason?"

"Yes."

"I see. Then I assume you are accepting my proposal."

"We need to go over the fine print."

"Very good, Elizabeth. I'm pleased you've finally come around. I'll pick you up at seven and we'll dine at the Greenridge Inn, since we were just at the club yesterday.''

"Mason, I'd rather not—"

"Elizabeth," he said crisply, "get over him."

The phone went dead in her hand. In spite of everything there were tears in her eyes when she put down the receiver. Of course Mason understood the irony of having her officially accept his marriage proposal beneath the very roof occupied by the man she loved. *Had loved*. No, why not admit it? She did love Cade. Oh, she hated him as well, but the line dividing the two emotions was only the breadth of a hair. Regardless of her feelings, the relationship was over. There was no going back. Too much had happened that was ugly and unforgivable. On one level a layer of unquenchable passion would always exist, a space where their souls might meet in some dream realm, but in the real world there was an imaginary point of no return that once crossed could never be renegotiated.

The faces appeared before him one after the other, just as Cade had known they would. Hope was etched on each man and woman's face, that this would be a new start for them, a step into a future providing better times. All of them were defectors from Elizabeth's mill, lured to his side by higher wages and the promise of a more efficient management to provide employment security. These people did not care for honor, nor were they bound by sentimentality associated with the old guard of Greenridge, who were hell bent on perpetuating the economic and social class structure of a bygone era. They just wanted to eat. It was all they had ever really wanted, merely to eat and sleep and raise their children with a semblance of dignity. His father had wanted nothing more and had fought hard to get it. Different times were here, however.

His scheme to avenge his father's defeat had been planned and executed flawlessly. He could congratulate himself on matching their guile and cold-bloodedness.

Except for one great error he had made. And this blunder spoiled the sense of victory which would have been his. He should never have fallen in love with Elizabeth.

Mason put down the telephone. So, one down; he had bagged Elizabeth. That was a relief. It had given him pause for concern, this new personality of hers. Who would have imagined she'd have hung on to the mill even this long? Well, that was the end of that chapter. She'd be married and under his dominion soon enough, and what she said and what she did would be exactly in accordance with what he required of her.

She might even like her new life. It would certainly be busy enough. They'd move into her house, of course. It was a perfect setting for a future governor. Naturally there would be parties—lots and lots of entertaining. They'd begin to travel throughout the state as he got more involved. And they'd have three children. With any luck they would look like Elizabeth and not him. She was a beauty.

The thought of having her to himself in bed was pleasant. He had never allowed himself to become overwhelmed in sexual matters as it diverted his energies from what was most important—his climb to the top of any mountain he set his sights on. He imagined she would be an exciting bed partner, and he would make an effort in that area himself. He was under no illusion that theirs would be a marriage of affection. But sex and emotion had little enough to do with one another.

There was one niggling aspect with which he had yet to deal, however, and that was the matter of Cade Delaney's destruction.

A simple enough matter.

Mason unlocked the side drawer to his desk. Opening it, he withdrew three file folders. He spent two or three minutes reviewing the contents of each report for information pertinent to his scheme. Confident in his selection, he reached for the telephone and dialed the number of the first of the three people who would become his co-conspirators in his bid to do away with the nuisance of Delaney.

Elizabeth had thought of dressing in black for the occasion, but at the last minute decided she would wear a white suit, in keeping with the sacrificial rites being celebrated that night.

Mason picked her up promptly at seven, just as he had said. He was dressed in a brown and beige pin-stripe suit, a pale yellow shirt and a richly colored paisley tie—the new image of banking, she supposed, conservatism with a touch of dash.

Except for Mason telling her that she looked very lovely, which she already knew, and her accepting the compliment in the flattest of monotones, they did not speak during the drive to the Greenridge Inn. For that she was grateful, it spared her the pretense of civility.

However, upon stepping across the threshold of the Inn, Mason's personality underwent a metamorphosis. His arm slipped possessively about her waist as he guided her through the portal, and a smile as wide as the

Mississippi fell into place when they were greeted by the hostess.

It took them several minutes to be seated. Their first pass was through the cocktail lounge, where Mason paraded about gathering goodwill, and then into the dining room, where several others were already enjoying meals. Curiosity lit each person's glance as Elizabeth dutifully followed along. She was not overly gracious, but she did manage "nice."

"So," Mason said, after they were seated and the waiter had appeared and disappeared with their order for drinks, "you have something to tell me."

Elizabeth couldn't help but smile. He was so sure of himself. He was so smug. "Yes," she began. "Obviously it would be in my best interests to marry you, Mason. That much is perfectly clear to both of us."

Mason nodded.

"However, there will be an understanding between us about certain issues. Otherwise, no deal."

"Elizabeth," he said coldly, but with a pleasant enough expression, lest anyone be watching, "I hardly think you're in a position to dictate terms."

"Come on, Mason," she scoffed, beginning to enjoy herself. "You and I both know how important I am in your little scheme of social elevation. I'm the pivotal prop in your grand performance."

"You lend a certain charm—"

"Credibility is the word. My family has stood for something in this state, longer than yours has even been in this country. My house, my name, even the way I look is the best package you're ever going to put together—unless you find some other means of extortion to use over some other poor soul down on her luck."

"That's enough," he said frigidly.

"Not nearly." She took a sip of her water. "Now then, Mason, this is the way things are going to be. I will continue on with the mill. I will be in charge."

Dumbfounded, he could only stare.

"Yes, you heard me right. Think of it this way: having your wife running such a big and important enterprise will make you look good. You'll appear so modern and strong. The new breed of man. That ought to get you a whole lot of votes from the 'libbers.'"

"I'll consider it."

"You'll do it. Or you can find yourself another bride. And there's one more thing, Mason. You and I will have separate bedrooms—"

"We are going to have children."

"You are going to have children, not me. I will not bear a child for you. And I will not let you touch me. Take it or leave it."

The waiter brought their drinks. Elizabeth was feeling wonderfully powerful, and cast him a dazzling smile that had the effect of distressing Mason far more than her last statement.

"I will not have you sleeping around," he said.

"I'm touched by your jealousy," Elizabeth said acidly. "Don't worry, it will never be said that the wife of Mason Philips is a slut."

"I have no intention of living a life of abstinence."

"Frankly, Mason, I don't care if you chase women or butterflies. I don't give a damn about you or what you do. All I want is to save my family's mill and the property I've got left. You do your part, I'll do mine. Agreed?"

"So," Mason said, "you've certainly become a very tough lady, haven't you?"

"You've got it. Have your lawyers draw up something legal that is in my best interests to sign."

He merely stared at her. Then he reached inside his jacket pocket and pulled out the little blue box again, opened it, and said, "Put your hand out, Elizabeth."

She waited a beat, then obliged. Her hand was trembling slightly as slowly Mason slipped the ring on her finger. "Look happy, damn you," he said.

"Do you know how much I loathe you?" Elizabeth returned, but the regulation smile was on her face. A deal was a deal.

Mason did not answer. Instead, he rose, and beckoned to someone who had just entered the dining room. Elizabeth looked, and the smile she had been wearing cracked into a million pieces.

Cade was standing in the doorway.

"Damn you!" she glared at Mason as he sat down with the smile of a man who had waited until the very last to deliver the crippling blow of defeat.

"Oh, my dear Elizabeth. You have no idea. Ah, Mr. Delaney, how nice that you could be here to celebrate the happy occasion of our engagement."

Chapter Fifteen

Cade gave away no emotion. But then he had been prepared for the meeting, Elizabeth considered, not like her, to whom the event unfolding was a horrible waking nightmare. She also saw that she had been very wrong to underestimate Mason. He was absolutely ruthless and far more clever than she had thought. Looking at him across the table, she realized suddenly that he was a man capable of anything, and as Cade slipped into the empty chair, she felt a frigid fear for the man she loved. It was perfectly clear how much Mason hated Cade.

The concern she was feeling must have registered in her expression, for Cade caught her glance, and for the barest moment their eyes connected and held in a communion of understanding that neither of them had ever really wanted things to get so far out of hand. Miserably, Elizabeth broke the bond and reached for her wineglass. The gesture was abrupt and so disordered that the glass tipped and spilled. A red stain began to spread out on the white tablecloth. The three of them stared silently at the spot. It reminded. Blood and death on a hot summer's afternoon had led to the meeting at this table.

Mason raised his hand for a waiter, who promptly scurried over to sop up the damage and place a white napkin over the stain.

She was pleased that Cade had not dressed for the occasion. While other men were stuffed into suits and starched shirts, he looked the way she found him the most attractive, casually attired in jeans and a brown leather jacket, a nubby cream-colored sweater beneath. Mason, although firmly in control, seemed stiff, his movements jerky in comparison to Cade's natural grace and ease of being.

"So," Mason began, once the waiter had completed his job, "it was good of you to join us for our little celebration."

Elizabeth flinched. "Mason, I refuse to be a part of—"

"Elizabeth and I," Mason overrode, "are going to make a splendid team. Each of us has something valuable to bring to this union."

Cade allowed himself a slanted smile, and nodded to Elizabeth. "I'm sure you two will be ecstatic together. A match made in heaven."

Elizabeth withered beneath his glance. She felt like a trapped butterfly, each man a pin on one of her wings. Cade finally withdrew his attention to address Mason.

"Okay, what's the game? I'm tired, Philips. I've had a long day, and if you don't mind abandoning the cheap theatrics, I'd like to get down to the real purpose of this little get-together."

Mason reached into his jacket's inside pocket and drew out a bulky envelope. He flipped it onto the table before Cade.

For a beat, Cade stared down at it then, as if bored with the whole drama, opened the packet. Elizabeth watched his face change from placid to stunned. When he looked up finally, she saw the veiled panic behind the calm facade he presented to Mason and her heart went out to him. Hadn't she so recently been in the same place herself?

"You can't do this," Cade said evenly.

"I have done it," Mason replied.

"It's not legal."

"Those are legal papers. And you had better abide by them or you're going to find yourself paying the price for defying the law."

"Mason . . ." Elizabeth broke in, panicked herself, understanding that something dreadful was being perpetrated against Cade, but not knowing what. "What are those papers?"

Mason turned to Elizabeth and calmly, as if speaking to a child of dim wit, said, "Those papers, my dear, are orders of condemnation against the mill run by Mr. Delaney. Unfortunately, our building inspector, a man of high esteem and total honesty, has deemed the Phoenix Mill an unsafe structure. It's a terrible shame, of course."

"Then he can fix it," Elizabeth said.

Mason looked peeved that she had so obviously chosen the wrong side to defend. "No, Elizabeth, he can't fix it. Not ever. The problems with this mill are insurmountable. Aren't they Mr. Delaney?"

Cade pushed himself from the table with enough force to knock his chair to its side. Either he was too angry to see the waiter, or too furious to step aside, but he crashed into the man, sending a tray of soup bowls flying to the carpet. Amid the gasps and cries of astonished diners, Elizabeth leapt up and, negotiating around the liquid mess and broken crockery, rushed after Cade who was already half up the stairs on his way to the second floor. Dimly, she heard Mason calling her name.

She didn't stop. Even so, she could not match Cade's furious pace and arrived at his room, just as the door slammed in her face.

"Cade!" she called, beating on the door with her fist. "Cade! Please, let me in. I want to talk to you—"

The door swung open with as much violence as when it closed. He stood before her, his eyes deadly with barely checked violence. In the blackness of that look, she lost her ability to speak, and merely stared dumbly at him.

"We have nothing to say. Go back down to your fiancé. And don't ever come near me again."

"No, Cade..." she stammered, realizing he meant exactly what he was saying, and that he was beginning to shut the door on her again. Like lightning, she stepped forward and slipped into his room.

"Get out," he said. He moved as if to throw her out.

"No...no...Cade. Please, just give me five minutes to explain."

"You don't have anything to explain, Elizabeth. What could you possibly have to tell me that I don't already know?"

"I had nothing to do with what Mason's done."

"Really?"

Never had she realized how much contempt could be packed into one word.

"He's protecting his interests. His interest in the mill that he gets through marrying you."

"Yes, yes. I admit that," she rushed. "I see that. I admit that, totally. But I had no idea that he was going to pull something so underhanded as to—"

"Run me out of town?" Cade shook his head. "How stupid, how naive can you be, Elizabeth? Have you no idea of the lengths men like Mason will go to protect their interests?"

"I know it's unfair—"

"Unfair? Elizabeth, you beautiful, misinformed hothouse plant, physical beatings and fires and—" Suddenly Cade broke off. His eyes went a strange color of slate green as his thoughts spun off into some other direction far from the room in which they stood.

"What?" she asked. "What are you thinking now?"

He looked at her then. "Some people are capable of anything."

"You think that of me? That I'd be capable of doing something—"

"All right. You want to know what I think? Fine." He took two steps closer, then stopped, as if to advance any farther would be dangerous. His eyes were filled with something other than the hatred of a moment before. There was a violence still, but it was of a nature more indicative of extreme sadness, belonging to a man who had lost everything and everyone he had loved in one motion. Even the voice he spoke in was curiously different to her, sounding at once like the Cade Delaney she knew and like someone else, a younger man of shattered idealism perhaps, who still existed somewhere beneath the polished persona.

"Once, Elizabeth, maybe you didn't know anything. You were just...just—" he made an expansive sweep of his arm, including the room, and from what she could tell by his next words, everything in Greenridge "—a part of something you had inherited. I don't believe you could ever have been held accountable for anything you did or didn't do then, because you simply weren't enough of a human being to understand or do anything autonomous. You merely existed in a comfortable time warp provided by your family and then your husband."

"I know that...I understand all of that, everything you're saying," she said, glad almost to find this bit of common ground on which they might move forward together. It mattered nothing to her that the surface was littered with her life's mistakes, so desperately did she want him to understand that she was not a part of Mason's scheme to ruin the mill. "It's all true."

"Yes. All of it is true. And this is true as well, Elizabeth. For a brief moment in time, you became a real person. A genuine human being. You got right in there, right up to your elbows in the whole cesspool of Greenridge reality and fought for what you believed and against what you did not."

Tears were flowing from her eyes, cascading like tiny waterfalls over her cheeks. She began to sob quietly. Cade continued, ignoring her.

"And then you made a decision." He said bitterly. "You had to choose. The old way. Or the new way."

"Dammit!" she screamed at him through her tears. "Damn you! I had no other way. I chose Mason because what else did I have? I would have lost everything, everything, don't you see? My home. The mill. I don't know any other world than this one. It's all I know. What the hell do you expect of me?''

"Nothing."

She stared across the room at him. "You don't understand, do you?"

"No," he said, "I do understand. It's you who have no real idea of what you've done. Elizabeth..."

"Yes?" Her name on his lips contained the old tenderness. The sound came from a place in his heart he had shared with her during the nights they had lain together, hot with desire, but connected to each other in a way transcending mere flesh.

"Yes?" She waited for this last possible reprieve.

"Elizabeth!" Mason stood outside the door. "It's unseemly for an engaged woman to be in a man's hotel room. Get out. Now."

She hesitated.

"Now! Elizabeth."

She was looking to Cade, as if he might rescue her, but he had already made himself plain enough. Mason knew he was on safe ground. There would be no challenge from Cade Delaney over her honor, simply because none existed in principle. She had already dishonored herself by accepting Mason's proposal.

Hardly able to see through her tears, she stumbled past Cade to the door. As she passed, he said, "Be careful."

Surprised, she looked up at him, and had there been any doubt about his tone being sincere, his eyes mirrored the serious intent of his words.

It was Mason who closed the door after her, shutting Cade out of her life.

* * *

Of course there was not a thing he could do about the order of condemnation on the mill. Mason was backed up by the powers of the town. Cade knew that even if he had the audacity to pursue the wrongful deed to the highest branches of State government, he would meet with the same defeat. The good ol' boy network had channels extending along every highway and into every nook and cranny.

Just in case he had any further doubts about his days in Greenridge having come to an end, when he arrived at the Phoenix Mill the following morning, there was an official sign tacked against the front door forbidding the plant to operate. A Greenridge patrol car sat parked at the curb as further insurance that Cade get the point. When Cade glanced back to the officer, the man tipped his finger to his hat and grinned.

Small crowds of men and women who had shown up to work, eager to begin new lives at higher wages, milled about the front of the factory. Like flies stunned by a blast of insect spray, their voices buzzed in short dying spasms, as they attempted to fathom this latest downturn in their already gutter-level fortunes.

Cade gave a short, difficult speech. There was some ugliness, but in many of the faces Cade seemed to read a sort of vague comprehension that what had come down that day was not of his doing.

When the last person had left, Cade walked over to the patrol car and tapped on the window. "Tell your boss I'm not ready to leave town. Tell Philips a man who's got nothing left to lose is a dangerous man. Tell Philips he just made a big mistake."

The officer only grinned. Cade grinned back, then turned and strode to his car.

* * *

"Hello, Elva," Cade said, as her pale face came into view behind the screen door. Her other hand held tight to the door she had just unlocked after Cade had beaten on it for five minutes, intermittently calling her name. He had heard the radio playing when he first stepped onto the porch. When he had called her name, it had gone off. Certainly she was in there, and he had to talk to her.

"Go away," she said. "I can't talk to you." Her voice was as fearful as the look she cast over his shoulder.

"Are you afraid someone may see you talking to me?"

"I'm not afraid of anything. I just have nothing to say."

"Elva . . . please," Cade said, and grabbed at the screen door, opening it quickly enough to insert his foot in the doorway before she could lock him out. "I understand you're afraid. I'm afraid, too. Not just for you and for me, but for another person. Another innocent person, Elva."

She hesitated, and he knew he was getting through to her. If ever he hated himself, he did at that moment, because of course he knew what might happen to her. But really, he didn't have any choice in the matter. And neither did Elva, if she could see into the future. She thought she was safe, but she was not. "You don't want to have another woman hurt, do you?"

"No," she said unsurely.

"You know who I mean, don't you?"

"Yes." It was a whisper.

"May I come in then? We've got to talk, Elva. We must. Or eventually something else very, very bad could happen."

The door opened for him, and he stepped inside the darkened living room. Elva Buck was thinner than in the summer. Deep hollows underlined her eyes. She was shivering with fright as she locked the door.

Chapter Sixteen

Two weeks had passed since Elizabeth had agreed to be Mason's lawfully wedded wife. Since that time, mercifully, no real changes had occurred, as if Providence had at last decided to be kind, allowing her to ease into her ill fortune. Life simply droned on for her in much the same way it had before the capitulation. There were, of course, the routine days at the mill, days more profitably spent now that the employees had returned to work for their former wages.

Although Mason had ranted that she should decrease their hourly wages by ten percent, Elizabeth did not exact any penance from them. She was too soft, he had railed. The workers had to be kept in their places. All they respected was power—real or fictional, it made no difference. Now they were helpless; without her to rescue them they'd be collecting aid from the government. There would never be a more appropriate opportunity than the present to rub their ungrateful noses into that fact. She would not.

Now that they understood their respective positions in the relationship, Mason was beginning to let her into his mind. His rationale was apparent; he felt he had nothing to lose, and would instill in her a fearful respect of his priorities. To work at cross purposes to any of his plans would be dangerous.

Power, Elizabeth was beginning to learn, was a favorite word of Mason's. On that basis alone she had defied his advice to penalize the employees. He would never have any power over her; she might, if in her best interests, acquiesce to certain demands, but she would never, ever allow him to bully her.

Evenings were for the most part lonely affairs. When she could, she evaded all social engagements with Mason, claiming sickness sometimes, work at other times. The few occasions she could not avoid she endured by blocking out as much of the ordeal as possible. Maybe in time she would find a way to totally anesthetize herself against contact with Mason and his friends.

She wondered about Cade. She knew he was still in town and supposed it was to oversee the liquidation of his mill equipment. The merest thought of what Mason had done to him filled her with a dizzying revulsion.

In off moments she would find herself contemplating fantasies wherein she would rescue Cade's mill and together they would join forces, their good triumphing over Mason's evil. But of course these were only the wild flights of her mind and had no conceivable basis in reality. Cade despised her. She could not blame him. If only, though, he could understand her position. If only a thousand million things . . . none of which could ever be.

That same day, Mason himself delivered the news. At four o'clock he entered her office and spread the Greenridge Bulletin before her. On its cover was a smiling picture taken of them recently at a restaurant. The caption announced their marriage. The date was given as just before Thanksgiving. They would be honeymooning in the Bahamas. It was all there, her background, Mason's background, where they would live.

Elizabeth read everything as if the person in question were some other woman. She had not been consulted on the date, nor on the place they would honeymoon. Everything had been engineered by Mason alone. She looked up. "Nice, Mason. Couldn't you have even consulted me?"

"To what purpose?"

"Oh, no reason. Except that maybe it's my life."

"Let's be frank. You don't want any part of this, anyway. So I just took the sting out of it for you and handled all the details."

"You're right. Absolutely. Thanks. Now maybe you could be so kind as to find someone to stand in for me for the rest of my life, too," she said, and was about to return to her work when her eyes fell upon another piece of information farther down on the front page. The hearing on her husband's murder had been set for a week away. Roy Buck had pleaded guilty, so it was less a trial than a mere formality to sentence him. It was not necessary for her to attend the ghoulish exercise, but she would, if for no other reason than to officially close a chapter on her life.

"Also," Mason said, "I'm planning a large celebration. Formal. We'll announce our engagement to our friends at—"

"I have no friends in this town."

"At the club," Mason finished, ignoring her. "The press will be there from the city. If things go right, I might even be able to get a television crew to cover the event. What will you wear? It's important you look absolutely perfect. White," he said, suddenly inspired. "You look striking in white. The impression of innocence can never be overdone when it comes to the media. People like to imagine it exists. White," he said again, pointing his finger at her.

Elizabeth smiled. She'd wear black.

Cade stood before the small desk in his room at the inn and stared down at the newspaper. Splashed across the front page were the two smiling faces of his tormentors. His blood turned molten and coursed through his body, its flow dissolving the last vestiges of illusion that in spite of everything Fortune would somehow set things right between him and the woman he loved. Overcome with love and loss, with hate and the urge to hurt those who had caused him such anguish, he knocked the paper to the floor.

His arm came up as if to strike violently at a foe, then instead curved inward, and he covered his eyes with his hand instead. For some time he stood like that, unable to think, incapable of moving, stunned by emotions long ago buried, rising wave upon wave from out of a bottomless abyss of pain.

Some other voice rose up in him, some other voice that had never cried out with fury, streaked up through his guts like a hot rod, its force tearing through the years of carefully controlled emotion. Staggering, he made it to the bed and fell backward on the mattress, incapable anymore of holding back the feelings with his rational mind.

Somewhere in the maelstrom the answer appeared like glowing words on a floating ribbon of calm. He would have what *he* wanted, what *he* wanted for himself—not to avenge his father's broken life, not to assuage his guilt, not to strike a blow in the name of universal justice—but simply because *he* wanted something for himself.

In the morning, when he awoke, he no longer felt like a shattered man.

To Elizabeth, Mason and all of his friends took on the appearance of one single person, one continuous being with the same false smile plastered on their identical faces, with the same regulation empty eyes devoid of any feeling deeper than the crackers they held. Mason and her friends looked to Elizabeth like the walking dead. But then, she quickly reminded herself, it was she, not they, who had expired. Perhaps being deceased was actually no more than a relative state, some contrivance of the mind. The living saw the dead as still and quiet; the dead saw the living in the same way. Perhaps there was actually no difference one way or the other?

Elizabeth was feeling the champagne, and in the vague way one knows when one is getting drunk and doesn't care, she realized she had already gone too far along the road to inebriation. She was already in dangerous territory. The next footfall could very well be on a land mine. The hell with it, she thought cheerily, raising her glass up to her eyes and viewing the world through a filmy, bubbly world of pale liquid.

"Elizabeth, that's quite enough."

"Hmmm?" Squinting, she continued to peer through the effervescent screen, but changed her view to include Mason.

He was smiling. But it was a false smile. She could see that, even if no one else could. If a shark smiled, it would look like Mason.

"You've had enough to drink, Elizabeth."

"Yes. I know. We agree at last, Mason. Do you think that augurs well for our marriage? That we finally, at last have a meeting of the minds?"

"Come, Elizabeth. We must talk." He removed the champagne glass from her hand and placed it on the tray of a passing waiter. Then he grabbed her firmly by the elbow—although no one watching would have suspected the pressure being exerted by his hand—and began to lead her to a quiet hallway off the club's main ballroom.

"Did you say talk or walk, Mason?" Elizabeth giggled, not so much because what she had said was that funny, although it did seem lightly amusing, but because she knew she would annoy Mason. She very, very much enjoyed that. If anything were to be enjoyable during the next few years, it would be this wonderful psychic guerrilla warfare she could wage against him. It could even provide her with a reason to live.

Now, even as her head spun crazily as she passed by all the walking, smiling, blinking, chattering dead people at this wake of an engagement party, Mason was reprimanding her under his breath. She was to behave herself at least for the duration of the formal announcement. "I want you looking and behaving like a queen," he said peevishly, while smiling into the sea of future supplicants.

He had brought her around the bend into the hallway. Elizabeth slouched against the wall. His smile vanished.

"You know, I could just kill you," he said, eyeing her up and down. "I told you to wear white, and you put on this black gown purposely, didn't you?"

"Guilty," she said, "but with an explanation. I didn't know this was to be my coronation. I'd thought it was a beheading. In that case, black's always more appropriate."

"Don't be cute, Elizabeth. I warn you. Tonight is of utmost importance to me. If you haven't noticed through your champagne stupor, there are television photographers who have recently arrived. I had to pull a lot of strings to get them here, and I don't plan on making a spectacle of myself. Is that perfectly clear."

Elizabeth simply stared. Then she said. "You make me want to vomit, Mason. And yes, everything about this evening and you and our lousy, stinking relationship is perfectly, crystalline clear."

Mason glared, but had too much at stake to risk a scene. "Come, Elizabeth, we'll discuss your various dissatisfactions at another time. For the moment, let's just get this over with."

Together they walked back into the crowded room. Mason led her straight to a small dais with a microphone positioned at one end of the large room. The room fell into a hush.

All eyes were on them. They stood together like plastic figures on the top level of a wedding cake. A crystal chandelier showered light upon the scene. For her own sense of personal dignity, Elizabeth decided to rise to the occasion and stood with a straight spine, the black crepe evening gown falling in graceful lines to the floor, the diamond drop earrings a compensation for the missing glitter of her smile.

Mason lifted his champagne glass in the air. A waiter promptly appeared and discreetly offered a filled glass to Elizabeth. Her fingers curled around its stem, holding it in a death's grip as Mason cleared his throat.

The first syllable of his practiced speech had barely left his lips when a series of shouts burst over his voice. At the far end of the room, the double doors flew open wide and Cade Delaney stood spread-legged in the portal.

Elizabeth gasped, but her own surprise was drowned by the collective gasp among the other spectators as Cade began a slow, studied, dangerous, assured stroll the length of the room. The town's elite dissolved back, out of harm's way, allowing him to cut a clear swath through their midst.

Along with the others, Elizabeth watched in frozen fascination, mesmerized by the spectacle of the handsome, unshaven man in jeans and leather jacket moving toward the dais as if he and not Mason commanded the occasion in progress.

Cade's eyes locked onto hers, and held her captive. Only when he reached the small dais on which she and Mason stood, did he move his attention to Mason.

"She's not marrying you," Cade said.

"Get out of here," Mason returned. "This is a private club and a private function. You don't belong here. You're not wanted."

"Neither are you, buddy, neither are you." Cade flicked his glance back to Elizabeth. "Is he, Elizabeth?

Do you want this man to be your lawful wedded husband till death do you part, Elizabeth?''

"Cade," Elizabeth breathed, her heart pumping madly with fright and joy, "this is crazy."

"Elizabeth? I believe all the people are waiting. Mason here is certainly waiting. And I'm waiting."

"No," she said, still looking at Cade, as if her power to speak came from the green force of his eyes. "I don't want to marry you, Mason. I never did. I never once loved you. And I never will. I'd rather die than be your wife."

Cade smiled slightly and so did Elizabeth. It was a crooked smile, due to the champagne, but nonetheless she felt happier than ever before in her life.

Cade offered her his hand. Slowly, deliberately, she took it and together they moved through the silent crowd.

At the door, she glanced back to where Mason stood like a statue, his face caught in a cross between a politician's smile and a rabid animal's snarl. Only then did Elizabeth note the lights and the small black machines with lenses leveled at him. Mason would be famous on the television news, just as he had always wanted.

Chapter Seventeen

They did not leave Cade's room in the Greenridge Inn for two days. Food, when they were hungry, was delivered to their door by room service. There were no outside interruptions to intrude upon their happiness. Nor was there any discussion as to his motives or her weakness. There was just the two of them, for two days, making love.

On the third day, Cade brought up the subject of reality. "You realize there's going to be a price to pay for all of this bliss we've found."

Elizabeth, who lay happily in the crook of his arm, merely sighed and stroked his leg. "Hmmm."

"My love," he said, and moved her hand away, "we've got to talk about what's going on out there beyond this door."

Elizabeth groaned and kissed his chest, but managed to pull herself up and shift her position so that they faced each other and said, "All right. Let's be sensible. Let's talk about the world and our place within it. I'm ready and equipped to fight dragons if necessary."

"Good. Because you may well have to, I'm afraid. Mason isn't going to exactly take what happened lying down," Cade said, at which point Elizabeth burst into a fit of uncontrolled laughter. Cade, caught up in the hilarity, joined her but finally asked why she was doubled up on the mattress with tears on her cheeks.

"Because..." she said, finally under control, and wiping her eyes dry with the edge of the sheet, "everything backfired on him. Even the television crew he had called himself, recorded the whole humiliating spectacle."

"Yes. And on that occasion, your dragon was hatched."

"You've got a point," Elizabeth replied, finally sober. "What's going to happen, do you think?"

"Well," Cade said, "I've already sold the equipment for my mill to another outfit, so I've got some cash to play with. Not an enormous amount, but enough to get your joint out of the red for the time being. And I'm willing to help you with the management—"

"Okay," Elizabeth agreed readily. "But I'm not taking charity. As long as I'm back on the track of being my own person, you'll be getting a fifty percent share of the mill—for good or ill. The money you put up to bail me out of this immediate mess will be taken out of my half of the profits until everything's cleared up. Basically, I'd say you're getting a raw deal, Mr. Delaney. I somehow doubt your business acumen."

"I've got you in the package as collateral, Mrs. Hart."

"Yes, you do," she said softly. "Yes, you do."

If they had expected trouble right away, they were disappointed. Mason had gone into some form of semiretirement. He'd even departed the bank on a temporary leave of absence, which was wonderful for Elizabeth. It allowed her to pay all the back loan fees to Mason's reasonably agreeable substitute.

Within a week of having Cade working alongside of her, the entire mood of the factory had been elevated a hundred notches. He was, as far as everyone including Elizabeth was concerned, a true genius at organization. And charm. Cade personally called every vendor and negotiated new terms with them, having new supplies shipped and obtaining an extension of credit based upon his projections of the future.

In the evenings, they would return together to Elizabeth's house, exhausted but nevertheless excited by their accomplishments.

"We're going to make it!" Elizabeth shouted one night while they prepared dinner together. "Oh, Cade...my love...my hero...we are going to come through this whole miserable thing. It's going to be sunlight and—"

"Steak," Cade said, plopping a couple of filets onto the plate she held out.

The following evening, she was in the same place, by the same stove, lifting fried chicken out of the same pan, when all the good times came to an end.

She caught the phone on the third ring, thinking it was Cade saying he'd been detained. With one hand flipping the browning chicken, and the other holding the plate, she kept her chin clamped over the receiver. "Hi...don't tell me...one of the machines is on the blink and you'll be there repairing it until midnight— What? Oh, no . . . oh my God! Oh my God, my God . . . No, I'll be right there.''

For a moment she felt faint. Then, bodiless with fear, she stumbled through the house, seeking car keys and purse.

In half an hour she was in the hospital. "I've got to see him," she said, trying to push her way past the doctor.

"Not yet," he said, holding her back.

"Damn it! Let me go to him!"

But she was held back by two strong masculine arms, which supported her as she fell sobbing against his green smock.

"He's in a lot of pain. It was a terrible beating. But there's no real permanent danger that we can see yet."

"Who did it?" she asked, her eyes stinging with fury. "Who did it to him?"

"That's a question the police will have to answer."

The next day, after being allowed to visit Cade, who was heavily sedated against the pain of his injuries, she made a trip to the police department.

"Who do you think did this?" the captain asked, as Elizabeth sat in his office with the door closed.

"Mason Philips," she replied with deadly calm.

There was a space in which disbelief registered in the police captain's face. "Mason Philips? Surely you can't be serious. Mason Philips is not a thug. In fact, from what I understand he's out of town."

"Mason Philips," she said again, adamant. "If he didn't do it bodily himself, then he was responsible for seeing that those men attacked Cade."

"We'll certainly look into—"

"No, you won't. You have no intention of doing that. For all I know, you were one of the men!" She stepped to her feet, and started to the door.

"Mrs. Hart!"

Elizabeth turned.

"Please . . . I'll do what I can to investigate what you said. But we both know this town. We know if things are meant to be kept secret . . ."

"Yes," she said, this time with less hostility, responding to the sincerity in the man's voice, "I know. But you check anyway," she said. "Please."

"You have my promise."

Cade returned home after a full week in the hospital, but even where there weren't bandages he was still sore and black and blue. The doctor said he might have been killed by the beating. Allegedly, there had been seven men. By the looks of the debris after the brawl, Cade had held his own.

"We're going to leave this town," Elizabeth said, when she had Cade lying in her big bed. She had brought him a hot bowl of soup and placed the tray on the nightstand. "If it happened once, it will happen again until he kills you."

"What's the day?" Cade asked.

"November seventeenth," Elizabeth answered. "We can make a life for ourselves somewhere else."

"The sentencing of Roy Buck is on the twentieth."

"What are you thinking?"

"That if there's a God, then justice will be done."

"And if there isn't?"

"Then we've got real trouble."

On November twentieth the courtroom was packed. The sentencing of Roy Buck was high drama in a town that thrived on any whiff of gossip. Murder filled the bill nicely.

Elizabeth had dressed in a blue wool suit and a red blouse. Her hair had been cut to just above her shoulders and fell in a sleek undercurve, framing her face. Everyone murmured as she took her place in a front row. Cade had wanted to accompany her, but she refused to let him leave the house. As it was, he needed crutches to hobble about, and he was still under pain medication.

Across from her, on the opposite side of the aisle, sat Elva Buck twisting a handkerchief through thin fingers. Although it was a wintry day, she wore nothing more than a thin cotton dress, more suitable for summer, and a scraggly sweater. Her complexion was sallow, with small sores on her face, which Elizabeth recognized as evidence of a poor diet and an excess of nerves.

Elizabeth felt the woman's eyes follow her as she slipped into her seat at the end of the row. Elizabeth turned and their eyes met—the widow whose husband had been struck down on a beautiful summer's afternoon, and the sister of the madman who did it, and who, on this bleak winter's morning, would undoubtedly soon lose his right to freedom forever. Fate's perfect symmetry, she thought, and looked away.

The proceedings began. Roy Buck, in handcuffs, was led out by the bailiff. The accused was a large man, lumpy and with broad stooped shoulders. His gait was a shuffle, and he looked down, not so much in shame, Elizabeth thought, but the way a man appears when he is not aware of the rest of the world about him. There was something pathetic about the human being before her, and in spite of herself a wave of sympathy obliterated the taste for justice that would have been more appropriate under the circumstances.

Elizabeth looked again to Elva Buck, whose attention she assumed would be trained on her brother; instead, the woman's eyes were turned to her. Quickly, Elva looked away, but not before Elizabeth had been left with the impression that there was something very desperate in the woman's glance that had nothing to do with her brother's fate.

The proceedings continued, rules of order being efficiently followed by the prosecuting attorney and the defense. Roy Buck was asked if he wished to make a final statement before sentencing. He said no, then nudged by his attorney, he remembered the correct response. Roy Buck stood on his feet, a blankness etched on his pale face.

At that same moment, there was a thump toward the back of the room. Then a thump-thump, and more thumps. Along with all the others, Elizabeth turned. Cade was coming down the aisle on his crutches. He looked monstrous, bandages and violent colors bleeding out from uncovered areas. Once, wincing in pain, he had to pause, and Elizabeth rose automatically to help him, but the bailiff shouted her down, and the judge beat his gavel against his bench and called for order. Cade thumped onward until he had come to the front of the court where Elizabeth was seated. She had moved over, making a place for him, but he did not at once take his place. Instead, he remained standing, and searched the sea of faces until the connection he sought was made.

Elva Buck stared back, her face even more pale. Cade did not move. He remained standing, and Elizabeth could feel the strain of his entire being directed to the frail woman in the opposite row. The judge was beating his gavel on his bench, and the bailiff was coming forward to settle the strange matter of disruption, when suddenly Elva Buck rose to her feet, and cried out in a low wail, "No! No! It's gotta stop here and now!"

Her entire body was trembling as she continued to half cry, half scream her anguished rambling message. The court was meant to be a temple of justice, and for once the rules of procedure were secondary to truth, expounded not in eloquence, but with the passion of rightness. Elva was allowed her speech.

"It was Mason Philips!" she wailed. "My brother killed Edward Hart, but it was Mason Philips who made him do it. He came up and planted the idea in Roy's head. And Roy—he was so sad and he wasn't working 'cause of being fired at the plant, and his head was never right anyway. Didn't really even know what was going on. Mason came to the house and he brought the gun and he paid Roy money to shoot Edward Hart. I was in the back—not supposed to be there. No one knew it. When I heard it, I ran. I ran and ran. I was going to tell the police to take care of Mr. Hart. Only Mason saw me. He caught me going up the road. And he beat me something bad. He told me he'd beat me every day until I was dead, and he told me he'd kill Roy if I ever opened my mouth. He said it didn't matter where Roy was. He'd kill him, and he'd come get me and my kids, too. I sent the kids away. Then he comes back to me and he says he's going to give me money now and then to help out, and I was to keep my mouth shut. But I felt so bad. I felt so bad..." And she looked at Elizabeth. "I went to tell you," she sobbed. "I went up to your house so many times. But I was afraid. And then Mason, he came and found out about it and beat me up again. But now...now..." She broke off into sobs, her finger pointing to Cade. "Look what he's done to him. He's a good man. He came and tried to help me. He was my friend, and I can't let this go on..."

Elva began to sink down, collapsing as if the words she had spoken were all that were inside of her to support her slight frame. Someone caught her in time.

"Oh...God..." Elizabeth said, and reached for Cade's fingers curled around the crutches.

"Yeah, he exists," Cade said in a low whisper, reverent and thankful as any prayer, as over it the judge was calling for an adjournment.

Chapter Eighteen

Thanksgiving.

And there was much to be glad for. Elizabeth placed the turkey on the table to cool and stepped back to admire her work just as Cade appeared in the dining room door. He was still multicolored from the fading bruises.

"Oh, hi! I didn't hear you come in. Were you able to find the leak in the water line?" she asked, wondering as she looked across the room at him, how she had ever thought to manage the mill on her own. However, it was good that she had at least tried, for in doing so, she could more appreciate Cade's genius at handling everything about the business with impeccable facility. And she sensed in turn that he admired her for what knowledge she had garnered on her own.

"I found it and managed to fix it temporarily," he said, coming over and giving her a light peck on the neck, which turned into a far more serious involvement when she turned into him and offered her mouth. His hands brushed over her hips with a liquid familiarity of the terrain, and as she reacted with more ardor, she felt him respond against her.

"What's that?" Cade said, drawing back a bit and sniffing.

"Oh...oh, God!" With a shriek, Elizabeth took to her heels and disappeared into the kitchen. "Saved!" she shouted, as Cade poked his head around the swinging door.

"Good. See what happens when you let your baser nature overrule reason?"

"Go shower!" she said. "And hurry. Everything's going to be ready in fifteen minutes. Oh, and tell the others." He saluted, blew her a kiss and disappeared.

There were still two boarders left. Elizabeth let them stay on, feeling protective of them. They were elderly and had made her home their own. She even felt guilty taking their money, but understood their sense of dignity made payment a necessity. The satisfaction of standing on one's feet was one thing she could understand. Financial difficulties had certainly eased up, although it would be another year until she could count herself totally solvent again. But all indications pointed to a renaissance of her fortunes.

Mason had certainly not experienced an upturn in his fortunes. Not only was he picked up by the state police on charges based on conspiracy to commit murder, but a Grand Jury investigation had been launched into other aspects of Mason's secret life. Many people came forward, all with interesting and frightening stories to tell of this one man's reign of terror. Of course Elizabeth knew full well it was not so much out of the goodness of their hearts that they stepped forward, but to save their own skins. Even the good ol' boys couldn't save Mason without hanging nooses around their own necks. And then there were many people who genuinely came forward to see justice done. These were the people who had been used and abused for so long, and who had lived in constant fear of Mason's power.

Well, good riddance to him, Elizabeth thought, and placed some flour in the bottom of a pan with turkey drippings to begin the gravy. Mason was finished business—or soon would be. His trial was almost over and before Christmas there would undoubtedly be a sentencing.

It was the best Thanksgiving she had ever had. It was the day Cade asked her to marry him. It was the day she said yes.

The Christmas tree sparkled with a magic that went beyond the two hundred bulbs and lights strung across its graceful branches. It reached twenty feet to the ceiling, and the golden angel at its crown had been a tight fit, the halo scraping the plaster.

Christmas carols played softly on the radio and a fire blazed in the hearth, before which Elizabeth was seated amid a jumble of Christmas wrapping paper and ribbons and gifts for Cade and their two elderly boarders.

Cade was at the factory. She had left early to get her wrapping done. There were only four days left before Christmas and she wanted the packages under the tree early enough to enjoy the sight for a little while.

Life was so good. Life was so beautiful.

"Hark the Herald Angels Sing," was playing when an announcer broke in with a local news bulletin. The jury had just handed down a life sentence to Mason.

The music took up again, the voices of the chorus lilting and joyous.

For a moment Elizabeth remained motionless, a strand of bright green ribbon caught between thumb and forefinger. The announcer's message kept echoing in her mind, and she sought to slow it down, to form some sort of emotional connection with the words she had just heard.

In the room, beside the hearth, with the lights of the Christmas tree glowing like the warmth from a hundred angels' hearts, Mason Philips and his dastardliness had little if any reality. She would tell Cade when he came home, if he had not yet heard the news himself, and then they would forget Mason forever. There was too much good in their lives to wallow in the negativities any memory of Mason dredged up.

Not ten minutes later she heard the sound of Cade's car, and rising quickly, scurried off to the hall closet with three gifts still unwrapped, hiding them behind a wall of coats and scarves and jackets. She was at the door, opening it for him, before he needed to go for his house key.

But it wasn't Cade. A stranger stood before her. In his hand was an envelope. "Mrs. Hart? Elizabeth Hart?"

"Yes?"

"This is for you. A little gift from Mason Philips."

The man turned and left Elizabeth holding the envelope with her name scrawled in pen over its front surface.

She closed the door and went back into the living room, where a new chorus was now singing about Frosty the Snowman. The fire crackled enthusiastically. The lights on the tree were every bit as bright. And yet the world had somehow grown darker for her as she sank into a chair and tore open the envelope.

My dear Elizabeth,

I have written this in advance of my sentencing, and have instructed it to be delivered to you immediately so that you, too, can share in whatever misfortune may be mine. For certainly nothing good can come out of my present circumstances. It is my whole intention to cause you nothing but pain, and yet what you will read will be the truth, the whole truth, and nothing but the truth. (Please allow me this slight irony. I have nothing left but irony.)

At any rate, you will be interested to learn that the man to whom you are so passionately devoted, is no better than myself. He is a liar, a schemer, a man bent on ambition at all cost, a user of beautiful women, and a clever deceiver whose sole motivation in being with you is revenge. I hope you appreciate my research. It took me quite a bit of trouble.

Elizabeth dropped the letter to her lap, her fingers burning as if she had touched flames. Her eyes jumped from the papers and moved through the room, fixing on nothing, seeking some sort of escape from their responsibility to complete what had already been started.

It was as if she were a heroine in a horror movie who hears a terrible noise in the basement of an old house. The audience knows she should run for dear life, get out, leave the horror unseen. But rather than escape, curiosity or some lurid spell takes over the mind of the heroine, and she remains, moving relentlessly forward to her certain doom.

Elizabeth's eyes fell again on the pages lying on her slacks. The unread words were there like some lurking fiend, waiting to be uncovered and wreak their destruction.

Her fingers closed around the edges of Mason Philips's missive. Nearby the fire snapped and crackled, and she looked to it, thinking herself at a crossroads. A flick of her wrist and she could continue on her course of uninformed bliss. Let the fire take Mason's words, whatever they were. Or, she could pick up the pages and educate herself.

No, she thought, she would not—could not—repeat her old ways, hiding her head in the sand when there was anything that smacked of unpleasant reality. Perhaps what Mason had to tell her was not even true. Maybe after reading it, she would find his allegations so ludicrous that she would laugh about it. Cade and she would sit before the fire in amusement, thinking of how ridiculous it was for Mason to think he could destroy what they had built between them with only a few words.

She picked up the papers.

Her eyes skimmed quickly over the words, then more rapidly, so fast that she found herself lost in a confusion of thoughts, questions, possible answers, more questions, and questions and questions, and would have to backtrack to make sure she had read correctly. The words were vile and disrupting and . . . true. They were true.

Elizabeth's eyes slid from Mason's signature to the engagement ring on her finger. It was a lie—the ring . . . the Christmas lights reflected in its facets...the chorus of "Joy to the World" softly filling the otherwise silent room. All of it was a hideous, cruel lie.

Cade stepped into the foyer and called out, "I'm starved. If you haven't anything on the stove, let's go into town."

By this time, he was in the living room. He stopped just inside the door, overwhelmed with the beauty of the scene. It was something out of his most cherished and fantastic dream. Only this was real. The lights on the Christmas tree danced and twinkled the season's merriment, and the fire was steady and warm. "Silent night, holy night..." sounded softly in the room. He was not a religious man by nature, but there was indeed something holy about the moment, and swept by gratefulness, he gave inner thanks to whatever force had guided him to this place and point in time. If Elizabeth had been there to greet him, the experience might have been overwhelming. He understood completely the expression "tears of joy." It was possible even for him to weep at such immense perfection.

"Elizabeth!" He was in the hall, crossing first to the kitchen, where he did not find her. Then back to the hall, calling again. Up the stairs he went, thinking that she might have fallen asleep. The door to their room was shut and he opened it gently, not wishing to disturb her rest but merely to satisfy himself that she was all right.

Instead he found her standing by the balcony's glass storm door, looking out over the front property. Then she had to have seen him arrive. And he knew then that something wasn't right.

"Hi," he said uncertainly.

When she did not respond, keeping her back to him, he came farther into the room. "Elizabeth? Is something wrong?'' She turned her face only slightly, but he could make out the hard line of her jaw, the extreme whiteness of her skin in the fast-fading natural light coming through the glass.

''I want you to pack your bags and get out of my house. I don't ever want to lay eyes on you again,'' she said.

He stood there, simply stood there, stunned for a long moment. ''I'm sorry. I don't understand. Has something happened? Well, of course it has. Something must have.'' He took a few steps forward. She might have stopped him with her voice alone, but her look of hatred as she turned was so complete, he knew better than to advance.

Her fingers were clutched tightly around some pages, and these she held out to him as she came forward. ''Here,'' she said. ''That's what happened.'' She passed by him, and at the door, she said only, ''I'm leaving now. When I come back here, I want you and everything that belongs to you gone.''

Torn, he wanted to grab her back to him, to sit down together and work through whatever the ridiculous and mysterious problem was, for certainly there had to be a mistake. But the sensible side of him knew that she was serious in what she had said, and that the answer to everything lay in the papers he held.

As the sound of her car faded down the drive, Cade began to read.

The house was the same as she had left it when she returned four hours later, except that the fire had died and there was yet another carol sounding sweetly through the downstairs. And Cade had gone. Everything of his had vanished along with him, just as she had ordered. A vast emptiness filled her. Not even hatred or remorse could have existed in that space. And that is what was finally so utterly frightening; she was without anything or anyone or any emotion, just this immense nothingness. She had never suspected that nothingness was actually something. It was. The horror of it was beyond words. It could only be felt and endured—that was the worst part, the endurance, because there was no running from it. The emptiness was her very self.

It was not until the next morning that she found his letter left on her dresser.

My darling Elizabeth,

Endearments are not natural to my nature, but the word in this case signifies exactly my feelings for you. I cannot expect you to trust me after what you have learned, but perhaps in telling you that everything that Mason said in his letter was true, you will see that I wish to be honest. Many times, I had wanted to come clean with you over the past, but finally when things were going so well between us, I thought I might escape the ugliness and confusion of all that came before. I can see now that this was a mistake. However, the truth is also that I always loved you. My feelings might have been taken for teenage infatuation by some, but no, it was always more. I loved you then; I love you now; I will always love you. Whatever we as individuals have had to work out on a daily basis—our many fights and misunderstandings—counts as nothing when I feel the connection our souls will always have no matter what the external situations. That is the real truth: that I love you, that regardless of your anger and hurt (all justified, given the outer circumstances), you love me, and that this love will last for all eternity. I leave you believing this with all my heart.

It was signed simply, "Cade."

A tear dropped against his name, and fuzzed the letters. Elizabeth wiped away others beginning to form. She stood there, knowing that what he had said was, in fact, the truth. He did love her. She did love him. And they would always love each other. Into eternity. It was exactly as he had said.

And yet, everything that had occurred and still existed in their relationship, denied these loving souls of theirs the opportunity to unite as a man and a woman who live and love in spaces of the real world.

Elizabeth walked to the French doors and looked out. A collage of shifting forms was superimposed against the terrain—her first view of Cade's car coming up the drive; the towering white clouds that had appeared every morning and built and built along with the summer's heat; the lightning storm in which a terrified Elva Buck stood beneath her window; and a thousand other impressions. Then, shifting from inner to outer, she saw the new homes off to the side, lined up with militaristic precision on property that had once been waving, natural grassland.

The past was gone. It was time for her to move on.

She worked swiftly. Brokers were hired for both the house and the mill. An attorney was retained to contact Cade, who had sent a forwarding address to her from New York, "In case she should ever want to reach him personally or professionally.'' There was still the matter of their joint interest in her mill. Her attorney informed Cade of her intent to place the mill up for sale, and requested certain papers be signed and notarized and returned by him in order that procedures could commence. He was further informed that thereinafter Mrs. Hart would no longer be in direct communication regarding the matter, as she was leaving Greenridge herself upon conclusion of the details initiating the sale of her properties.

Three weeks into January, Elizabeth visited her attorney for the last time. She would be leaving in two days for California.

"California?"

"Yes," she said, laughing at his surprise. She, in turn, was surprised that she had laughed. It wasn't often that anything seemed very amusing. "Isn't that where all the dispossessed go?"

"It's just such an unlikely place for a person like you to want to live," he commented.

"Precisely why I'm going. The tried and true certainly hasn't worked."

Her attorney looked downward, bit his lip slightly, and when he looked up, his words were measured and tentative. "I realize it isn't in my capacity to...to advise on your personal life—"

"You're right. It isn't."

He was quiet. Then having reconsidered again, he said, "I told Mr. Delaney as much. However, I feel I should tell you that Mr. Delaney seems genuinely concerned about your welfare, and perhaps..."

Elizabeth stood. "Thank you for your concern. The situation between myself and Mr. Delaney is quite over. As I've sold my car, I'm leaving on the eleven o'clock train the day after tomorrow. You'll have my address in California as soon as I have one."

On Thursday morning, with no more than a suitcase, she set off on the train to her new life. The idea of having nothing more than this suitcase with a few changes of clothes, was oddly exhilarating. It was the first time she had nothing but herself to rely upon. There would be no family props to support her; only herself. She felt as if by making the decision, she had gained a new self in losing the old one. The terrifying feeling of "nothingness" was now being filled with a sense of security—she was that security.

As the train pulled away from the station, she stared unseeingly out the window. She remembered how she used to lie awake nights waiting for Cade to come to her. Closing her eyes, she wished for those moments again, wanting to turn back time and be in his arms, wanting what she could never have again. This part of her life, like the other parts from which she had now been divorced, was over.

The train, which had gained momentum, and was speeding out of town, lurched to an unexpected stop. The curious rushed to windows, peering down the track, voices speculating excitedly on the truck pulled dead across the train's path.

The guesses ranged anywhere from an old-fashioned train robbery to a man who'd suffered a heart attack.

Elizabeth returned to her private thoughts, and in a minute was an island unto herself, untouched by the outer commotion.

"Stop him! Stop that man!" came a shout from the far end of the car.

Elizabeth looked up to see Cade striding down the aisle toward her.

An angry conductor puffed along on short legs after him. "You just committed a crime!"

"And I'm about to commit another one," Cade said in a threatening voice. "While you're at it, mark me down for kidnapping."

Elizabeth had half risen, and was thinking in terms of escape, when he grabbed her wrist and jerked her into the aisle. "Come on, this is your abduction."

"No, Cade . . . Cade, no, I don't—"

"I'd appreciate a little cooperation," he said, overriding her protests as he dragged her down the aisle.

"You're mad. You can't do this!" Elizabeth objected, tugging in the opposite direction.

"If you haven't noticed, I *am* doing it," Cade replied with a laugh. "You can complain about it all you want at home," he said.

Amid shouts and threats from passengers who apparently thought him a lunatic too dangerous to tangle with, and conductors too baffled at the breach of civilized behavior to do anything effective, Cade dealt with her struggles and shoved her into the truck which still straddled the tracks.

"How the hell did you—"

"Find you?" Cade started the truck forward, waving to the angry bystanders still bustling about the sidelines. "Your lawyer. We guys like to stick together. Besides, as a man who hears his share of lies, he knows the truth when he hears it. He believed me when I told him I loved you and you loved me and that we were going to live happily ever after."

"This dramatic grandstand play of yours is not going to make any difference, Cade. It's over. It's finished. Completely."

Cade made a hard right, and took a road leading alongside the tracks. "I was thinking the same thing as I flew down here. We're over with the whole thing. Finished. And we finally won."

"You won. You managed to hoodwink me and eventually run me out of town. Wasn't that the plan all along?"

"We ended all the hate. We put a decent business together, where people of this town can get a fair shake. And we fell in love. If you don't call that winning, I don't know what it is."

"That doesn't change things."

"It changes everything. You think I'm going to let you throw something so good away?"

"I'm not throwing anything away—I'm going away. There's a difference."

"What the hell do you think you're going to find out there in some other city? California, right? There's a few million people out there who are searching for the same things there that they couldn't find in Iowa or Pennsylvania or wherever the hell they came from. It's all just more of the same, when it comes right down to it. I know. You can take your stand here, or you can do it somewhere else, sure—but ultimately it's your stand."

"Mason used me. You used me. You think I can just put all of that aside? That I can forget all that garbage you put me through!"

"Yeah, that's what I came here to do. I came here wanting your body—or so I liked to think. I came here wanting the mill. I came here wanting to settle old scores. But instead I found something new that was worth more than anything the past had to offer."

"Exactly," Elizabeth said. "That's why I'm leaving. Because I'm sick of the past. I don't want any reminders to clutter up my present."

"Okay, okay. You want to get out of town, fine. But we leave together then. The hell with the house, the hell with the mill. It's you I want. It's now I want. And I'll take it any way it's offered. And anywhere it's offered. If I've got to make love to you in the middle of an orange grove, so be it."

The road they followed continued to run parallel to the railroad tracks. To the left, Elizabeth saw the rolling fields, and peaks of houses nestled in the hills off in the distance. Trails of white smoke drifted from a chimney here or there. Her mind slipped back again, carrying her into the sensations of her girlhood, and in a fleeting instant she traced the joys and sorrows she had known during her life in Greenridge.

"What was it like," Elizabeth whispered, looking to Cade, "that day you left town on the train with your father?"

"Hell . . . a slice of hell," Cade said, a tightness coming over his features. "It was leaving pieces of myself behind. This was my home, Elizabeth." He cast her a quick look. "For better and then for worse, Greenridge had been the only home I'd ever known. I was sad. I was scared on that train. It was the coldest day of my life."

"And then you came back."

"Yeah. I had to. I left the best parts of me here. Had to get them back again. You change locations, but you can't run away. That's the bottom line."

The train she had been on, raced by. There was a steady blur of little faces staring at her from the windows.

"I guess unfinished business keeps pace," she said softly.

"Dogs us down every highway," Cade said, glancing at the train. "A real pest."

Elizabeth nodded, then sat for a moment absorbed in her own thoughts. The train had raced on ahead without her on board. She placed her hand over his, and said, "Let's go home," she said. "Together...for good."

The road took another turn, and Cade guided the truck away from the tracks that led out of Greenridge. Elizabeth's hand was still on his. She squeezed it gently, and when he looked he saw that she was smiling and crying at the same time. So was he.

Silhouette Special Edition

COMING NEXT MONTH

#385 FORBIDDEN FRUIT—Brooke Hastings
Noble Lady Georgina felt obliged to marry her social equal. But when her grandmother hired macho, working-class Mike Napoli to chaperone Georgina, attraction soon outranked obligation!

#386 MANDREGO—Tracy Sinclair
Elissa had vowed to avenge her father's ruin. Her plot led her to an island paradise—and into the arms of her enemy's bodyguard, dangerously attractive Troy Benedict. Could revenge possibly be so sweet?

#387 THE MIDNIGHT HOUR—Jude O'Neill
Sassy Cleo and wise-cracking Gus were once partners in mystery writing and marriage, but their famed collaboration had led to calamity. If they reunited, would they be crafty enough to write themselves a happy ending?

#388 THE BABY TRAP—Carole Halston
Ginny Sutherland wanted a baby—without the complication of remarrying. Still, she'd need a male temporarily, and virile Ed Granger might just be the man for the job....

#389 THE SUN ALWAYS RISES—Judith Daniels
Restaurateur Catherine Harrington didn't want to love and lose again, but wandering, "no-commitments" Nick O'Donovan was convincing her to take the risk....

#390 THE FAIRY TALE GIRL—Ann Major
When her fairy tale marriage failed, Amber Johnson left the Bahamas with her illusions destroyed. So how could she believe rancher Jake Kassidy's promise that with him she'd live happily ever after?

AVAILABLE THIS MONTH:

ATTRACTIVE, SPACE SAVING BOOK RACK

Display your most prized novels on this handsome and sturdy book rack. The hand-rubbed walnut finish will blend into your library decor with quiet elegance, providing a practical organizer for your favorite hard-or soft-covered books.

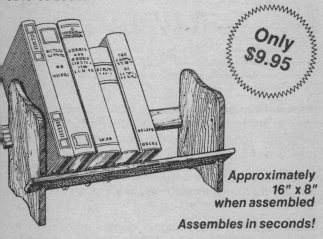

Only
$9.95

Approximately
16" x 8"
when assembled

Assembles in seconds!

To order, rush your name, address and zip code, along with a check or money order for $10.70* ($9.95 plus 75¢ postage and handling) payable to *Silhouette Books*.

Silhouette Books
Book Rack Offer
901 Fuhrmann Blvd.
P.O. Box 1325
Buffalo, NY 14269-1325

Offer not available in Canada.

BKR-2R

*New York residents add appropriate sales tax.

Silhouette Desire

Available May 1987

Still Waters
by
Leslie Davis Guccione

If Drew Branigan's six feet of Irish charm won you over in *Bittersweet Harvest*, Silhouette Desire #311, there's more where he came from—meet his hoodlum-turned-cop younger brother, Ryan.

In *Still Waters*, Ryan Branigan gets a second chance to win his childhood sweetheart, Sky, and this time it's for keeps.

Then look for *Something in Common*, coming in September, 1987, and watch the oldest Branigan find the lady of his dreams.

After raising his five younger brothers, confirmed bachelor Kevin Branigan had finally found some peace. He certainly didn't expect vibrant Erin O'Connor to turn his world upside down!

D353-1